A Man in Trouble

ALSO BY LON OTTO

A Nest of Hooks

Cover Me

Grit

A Man in Trouble

Stories by

Lon Otto

BRIGHT
HORSE
BOOKS

Brighthorse Books
13202 N River Drive
Omaha, NE 68112
brighthorsebooks.com

ISBN: 978-0-9908670-6-7

Acknowledgments

"The Urban Forest," *Prairie Schooner*
"Wrapped in Blue," *Water-Stone*
"Her Good Name," *Prairie Schooner*
"Furious," *Great River Review*
"What It Was," *Water-Stone*
"A Man in Trouble," *American Fiction*
"Feast of the Circumcision," *Water-Stone*
"Run," *Water-Stone*
"What Is *Son*?" *Prairie Schooner*
"Wider, Higher, Deeper," *Fifth Wednesday*
"Crawl Space," *Colorado Review*
"Such Fire," *Great River Review*
"A Small, Dark, Roaring Moon," *Blink Again*
(Spout Press)

Cover Photo: Dante Everett
Author Photo: Audra Otto

CONTENTS

For Kathleen

A Man in Trouble

THE URBAN FOREST

ALTHOUGH HE LIVED just two blocks from it, Corvin had journeyed into the Liberty Plaza housing project only once before. His son, in kindergarten then, had given a Hmong classmate a birthday party invitation. For a while the boy had stopped by almost every day on his way home from school to ask if they were going to have cake now, but Corvin had been afraid the boy's parents weren't aware of the party. For all he knew, they might not have spoken English.

The morning of the party, while his ex-wife decorated the house, Corvin and Willy had walked over to the housing project and asked the few people they met—some children, a fierce-looking grandmother with a baby lashed to her back in folds of cloth, some teenagers—if they knew where a boy named Pao lived. Willy didn't know his last name. No one could help them. A couple of times, Corvin had tried to describe the boy—an inch or two taller than Willy and three times wider, with hair that stood straight up in a dense black brush. Corvin couldn't tell if anyone even understood what he was saying. As they walked up and down the paths that wound among the brick apartment buildings and densely-planted vegetable gardens trellised with sticks and chicken wire and random salvaged objects, Willy had kept a tight hold on his hand. Foreignness wrapped around them like an electric skin. They had given up, finally, and a few weeks later Pao had ridden up to their front porch on a tiny bicycle and asked, was it time for them to have cake?

11

That had been four years ago. This time Corvin was alone, lugging a long-handled shovel and branch lopper and leather gloves and brand new pruning shears and pruning knife and heavy wire cutter, high-laced work boots on his feet, cowboy hat shielding his bald head and tender neck from the September sun. At the neighborhood video store a week ago, he had seen a notice for volunteers to help plant trees around the housing project, one of several places in Minnesota where hundreds of Hmong people had been settled after years in refugee camps in Thailand. He had left the office early today and come home in the middle of the afternoon, before his kids got home from school. He changed into old clothes and left a note saying where he was.

Corvin had done this kind of work before. The previous summer, he had shown up on a Saturday morning in a vacant lot on Selby Avenue, joining fifty other volunteers to plant hackberry trees in the boulevards along that street. The Minnesota Department of Natural Resources had supplied the trees, which were delivered by beefy, sun-burned college boys from a nursery, who dug the rough holes with a backhoe and next to each hole left a leafless tree lying on its side, its root ball wrapped in burlap and bound with ropes and cramped into a welded wire basket, branches trussed together with plastic ribbon.

Standing in front of the community jobs center, a guy from the DNR had given the assembled volunteers a speech about the urban forest, then demonstrated how to plant the trees. An argument had broken out concerning the wire basket, which was hard to cut once the root ball was down in the hole and almost impossible to bend out of the way in order to release the top of the burlap. One of the nursery boys insisted that the wire cage had to stay fixed around the root ball, or it would fall apart when they tried to lift it into the hole. An old woman who had been introduced as the Master Gardener supervising the tree planting grumbled to some in the crowd that the last time she had done it they had removed the wire first, which is what Corvin thought they should do, but she wouldn't confront the nursery boy, and the DNR guy wasn't sure, and the volunteers argued this way and that, with somebody every so often jumping down into the hole with the root ball and trying his hand at clipping the wire and wrenching it out of the way.

The DNR guy's little side-cut wasn't up to the job. Somebody went home and brought back a bolt cutter with yard-long handles, and that got the job done, though it was awkward working with it in the hole. Finally the nursery workers drove off in their big green truck and volunteers crowded in to shovel dirt back into the hole. Corvin moved down the street to work on a tree that was less mobbed.

Something had bothered him about the group of volunteers. It wasn't just that they were mostly white people in their late twenties and early thirties, it was the air of cheerful virtuousness that swirled among them. He liked the neighborhood's mix of races—black and Asian and white and Hispanic—and it was disappointing to be merely one more white face in this do-gooder crowd.

After the crush of volunteers around the first few trees, small groups had started to form and spread out. There were some forty trees sprawled along the boulevards on either side of Selby in front of the old frame houses, half-abandoned storefronts, cinder block churches, karate center, earthwork-protected grade school, vacant lots, drug store with pictures of windows and shutters painted onto its blank, bullet-proof brick walls. Corvin found himself working with a red-faced guy who said he was a retired DNR employee, a black guy with shaved head and a long beard, and the Master Gardener, an old white lady who reminded Corvin of his favorite aunt.

By their third tree, Corvin's group had worked out a system. Rejecting the nursery boy's opinion, they started by cutting all the way down one side of the wire basket and bending it away until they could pull it off completely. Meanwhile, somebody measured the root ball with a shovel handle and adjusted the backfill to the right depth, and the Master Gardener snipped the ribbons that bound the limbs together and pruned a few branches that didn't look right to her. Then the men heaved the tree upright, looped the web sling around the root ball, grabbed onto the four loose ends of the sling, braced themselves, and on the count of three lifted and swung it over and lowered it into the hole. The rest was easy—retrieving the sling, sawing through the ropes that trussed the root ball, peeling back the burlap and stuffing it down around the sides, half-filling the hole, watering with a hose from a tank truck that circulated up and down the avenue, filling the hole the rest of the way, finally surrounding the tree's base with shredded bark.

Among the rocks and loose dirt of every fourth or fifth hole, they would find rotting fragments of old burlap—graveclothes of a previous tree planting. They speculated that maybe the species had been something less hardy than these hackberries, or playing kids or a veering car had snapped it off before it was big enough to take care of itself, or its first summer might have been too dry and nobody had thought to run a hose out and water it. Some of the residents watched the volunteers skeptically. "Do this every couple years," a woman said from her front porch. "Goddamn waste of money."

Most residents had seemed glad to see the trees going in, however. When a shirtless old man came down off his porch at one point to complain that they were putting too small of a tree in front of his house, the retired DNR man went and got the mulch truck, and he and the bearded guy and Corvin loaded the unwanted tree into its bed and exchanged it with one that had been left in front of a car repair shop.

The work had taken longer than Corvin expected, and he was brutally sunburned by the end of the day, but he was proud to have been involved. And he was happy, now, to come to another tree planting, better equipped this time and knowing what to do from the beginning, happy at the prospect of working with his Hmong neighbors, still as alien to him as they had been four years ago, when he and Willy had gone looking for Pao. Four years, living two blocks away from them.

When Corvin arrived at the housing project, he saw that the nursery trucks had been by already, leaving balled and burlapped trees next to holes chopped into the boulevards surrounding the complex of brick apartment buildings. The trees were leafed out this time—something with shiny bark and spear-shaped leaves standing balanced on their root balls along the west side, and maples lying down on the south side, along Marshall Avenue, the front of the project, where the volunteers were supposed to meet.

No one else was there. A bunch of preschool kids were approaching from the other end of the block, surrounding two Hmong women wearing long, intricately-patterned blouses and skirts that swung just above their sandaled feet, their hair swathed in printed scarves. Before they reached him, the women turned aside, herding the toddlers between two of the apartment buildings and out of sight.

Corvin checked his watch. He dumped his tools on the grassy boulevard and wandered down to the end of the block. Along the east side of the project, too, the boulevard was lined with those shiny-barked trees. They leaned this way and that as the street slid down toward the freeway, but they were small enough to balance upright over the weight of their root balls, which were bound only with burlap and rope, free of the wire baskets that had been such a pain in the ass when planting hackberries the previous summer. There was welded wire clutched around the maples' root balls, though.

Corvin studied a little garden between two buildings, an arbor constructed from chicken wire, dead branches, pieces of plastic grill from a window fan, a broken hockey stick, electrical conduit, mop handle, coiled telephone cord, bicycle handlebars with handbrakes and cables still attached, the slatted side of a baby's crib. Jalapeños and onions and baby eggplant grew beneath the arbor, and some kind of squash vine was climbing over it, with long, pale green fruit dangling. The largest, big as a coffee pot, hung cradled in the bill of a faded blue Nike visor.

Finally he sat down on the curb, the two- and three-story apartment buildings of Liberty Plaza at his back. After a while, a DNR guy drove up in a yellow truck and explained that there was a service club for teenagers at the housing project, and they would be the main ones working on the planting. They must be still in school. He gave

Corvin the name of the woman who was in charge of the club, Lee, then unloaded shovels, rakes, pitchforks, and a couple of web slings, and drove off again to get a load of mulch.

It was a hot afternoon, more like midsummer than early fall. Corvin stretched out on the grassy boulevard and covered his face with the cowboy hat. For a while, every time a car drove by on Marshall he tilted the broad-brimmed hat to see who it was. But nobody stopped. He was right next to the sidewalk. The vulnerability of lying there stirred a thin buzz in his stomach and joints, itched behind his eyes. It was his neighborhood, and yet it was a foreign country, the air strange with unfamiliar cooking odors drifting out of the apartments, the ground vibrating with the footsteps of ghosts.

At a party a few months before, he had met a Nigerian woman, a writer visiting from New York. In an articulate, rational voice she had spoken of the Hmong as a race of opium traders, natural allies of the drug-dealing CIA. Corvin had felt disloyal to his neighbors, but he said nothing. He didn't know enough. Their situation was too strange to think about clearly. Farmers from the mountainous frontier separating China and Laos, what could they have thought when they arrived in Minnesota, in St. Paul? When the CIA recruited them to fight against the communists, what shaman could have had a vision strong enough to see those years in refugee camps, then this country, this northern, Midwestern state, this inner-city neighborhood, these balled and burlapped trees?

For a moment he didn't know where he was. Somebody was there, saying something. He must have fallen asleep. A woman was crouched next to him, her body radiating a perfume of salt and oranges. "Are you Corvin?" she said. "I'm Lee." A young white woman, with permed brown hair and large glasses.

He had been expecting a Hmong person. That was why he was here, to get to know some of them, who walked by his house every day but never exchanged more than a shy nod of greeting. So why this rush of happiness? She stood and helped him up. A dry, strong hand that sent electricity flooding into him. She was as tall as he was, dressed in a faded red T-shirt and khaki shorts, heavy socks and hiking boots.

"The kids will be here in a few minutes," she said. "Thanks for helping us. Steve said you were coming."

"Sure, I like doing this sort of thing." Steve was the DNR guy? "You know," he said, "I think we've met before."

She studied his face. "You look familiar, too," she said, without conviction. "You live around here? We've probably run into each other. I teach at Central." She reached out and took his wrist and turned it a little so she could read his watch. "They should be here by now." She walked down the sidewalk a few steps.

With the pressure of her fingers still burning on his skin, Corvin stood braced, holding his breath as a wave of longing rolled over him, tossing realization into the air finally like a glistening chip of wood. Susanna, his girlfriend in college. Lee was so much like her, the timbre of voice, that height, gray eyes behind those big, retro glasses, he could barely breathe, he could feel that frizzy hair pressed against his lips, the taste of her bitter smoker's mouth. Susanna. More truly her than she could possibly be herself by now, twenty-five years later, a mother, perhaps, as he was unbelievably a father.

He sat down on the grassy boulevard again, smelling the heat of southern California, the sweet rage of antiwar protests, the exploding word "Cambodia," textbooks grown weightless and inconsequential, sex in an emptied dormitory on an unmade bed, the bite of tear gas drifting across the quad.

And then everybody was there. The DNR guy, Steve, arrived with a truckload of shredded bark, and a knot of teenage girls emerged from somewhere in the housing project, followed by a straggle of other girls and a few boys. The kids were Hmong, mostly, though two of the girls were black. Corvin and Steve demonstrated the planting process with one of the maples. This time nobody questioned the wisdom of cutting off the wire basket before lifting the tree. When they had fastened the sling around the root ball, Corvin grabbed two of the handles, but the DNR guy called for volunteers, and a tall black girl who looked too fragile for the job leaped forward and took one of the ends from Corvin, and a solid-looking Hmong girl grabbed the third handle. With the DNR guy on the fourth strap, they lifted on the count of three, and to loud encouragement from the other kids they staggered to the hole and lowered the wildly thrashing tree till its heavy root ball rested on the backfill.

The two girls sprang out of the hole and chanted, "Girls rule! Girls rule!" to the boys who had walked up to the scene so casually you wouldn't have known they were a part of it. Work groups formed. Nina and Choa, the two who had helped with the first tree, and a square-built boy who looked like a grown-up version of Pao, whose name Corvin never did catch, and a Hmong girl everybody called Frenchie worked with Corvin, along with four or five kids who wandered in and out, now shoveling, now taking a hand with the wire cutter, now hauling hose.

Corvin kept an eye on the group Lee was working with. It felt like a cruel dream, her friendly indifference to him, their eyes meeting now and then but never locking, the first woman with whom he had ever been in love.

As he dug, as he threaded the sling together and heaved against the weight of tree and earth, he felt the ache throbbing from twenty-five years before, when they had clung to each other on that narrow dormitory bed and debated his flight to Canada, weighed in their mouths a year in prison, pressed their bodies against his single-digit draft lottery number like a tongue drawn to a broken tooth, feverish considerations that would be swept away forever by an epileptic seizure in the middle of the night two weeks later. He had woken in the infirmary, remembering nothing. "My son would give his left nut for this," the college doctor had told him the following week, after explaining his electroencephalogram results, a seismograph that had shaken Corvin's draft status from 1A down to 4F, medically unfit.

Nothing was the same after that. Susanna had joined the Peace Corps following graduation and was sent to the Philippines, and Corvin had gone back to Minnesota. He watched Lee now, towering over the Hmong teenagers as Susanna must have done among her Filipino villagers, and wondered mechanically, as he had for years afterward, why the left nut? He had never told any of this to Irene, the woman he lived with for two years, nor to Rachel, whom he had married, the mother of his children, who lived a few miles away now and kept the kids on alternate weeks. His left nut, an expression.

They finished the maples, then started on the Japanese lilacs, which is what the trees with the shiny bark turned out to be. Because the street sloped downhill so steeply here, it was hard to judge when the trees were upright, you had to line them up with a corner of the apartment buildings.

There were more and more people around—Hmong woman with their little children, school-age kids who liked to swing around on the narrow trunks and tended to wander off with tools, and some more teenage boys. He lost track of his pruning shears, then his shovel, but went on without them, caught up in a march that wouldn't stop for him to look around. A large boy who turned out to be Pao came by and remembered him and asked about Willy, then ran off with his friends—slight, delicate-looking boys who made Pao seem even more massive.

Corvin hadn't had anything to drink all afternoon and kept hoping that his son or daughter would come over to see how things were going, maybe offer to bring him a soda or something, even try to pitch in. Willy usually watched television when he got home from school, and Hannah worked on her homework. Corvin was thinking about them as he snugged up the sling and called for another lifter. Frenchie, slender but strong, and Choa, who had that solid build and could lift as well as any of them, were still there, but Nina and the sumo boy had gone off to rake mulch. One of the new boys, small and wiry, reached down and took hold of a strap handle. Corvin, Choa, and Frenchie each grabbed one of the other straps, and they lifted the tree on three and lowered the tree ball into the hole.

The new volunteer stepped back, lighted a cigarette, and talked in Hmong to a boy who had begun to shovel in fill dirt before Corvin had finished retrieving the sling. The two of them were older than the others from the club, Corvin thought. Then he realized that they were a lot older, not brothers to the teenagers, but fathers or uncles, his own age, maybe older. They were small, no taller than his ten-year-old son, which was what had fooled him at first.

Corvin looked around. More and more of the volunteers were these men, who must have been coming home from jobs, English language classes, bureaucratic offices. Their faces were carved and leathery, the skin of farmers, though they were dressed in city clothes—corduroys, double-knit pants, shirts with long collars that were fashionable a few years before, a Vikings jersey, a nylon Twins jacket.

The teenagers, meanwhile, were evaporating. Choa was gone, then Frenchie. He couldn't see Lee anymore. The Hmong fathers picked up shovels and moved to the next tree. Corvin brought the sling along and threaded it around a root ball, then went over and showed a man how far to backfill the hole, then ran back and reattached the sling that two men had been using to drag the tree forward.

He explained the procedure again, and couldn't tell how much anybody was understanding. Everybody was talking, five or six men crowding in sometime, taking hold of the tree anyway they could. He finally managed to get the sling back in place, two men took hold of a handle each, and Corvin grabbed the other two. "Okay," he said, "we'll lift on the count of three." One of the men started lifting early, sending the tree tilting back into Corvin's face, knocking off his cowboy hat. He laughed, trying to recover. "Not two and a half. Three. We'll lift on three." He counted emphatically and mimed the lift on three. The men nodded, and this time they managed a successful lift, swing, and lower, though the one guy was still a little early.

The hole hadn't been backfilled enough to raise the top of the root ball to grade. Corvin explained again how it was supposed to be and rocked the tree over so he could work more soil under the roots while several men shoveled dirt around it. He got out his pruning knife and started working on the ropes that secured the burlap. It was getting dull from sawing through the hard hemp. A man who seemed a little older than the rest, his face more deeply lined and his thick hair going silver, took the knife from him and stropped it on the worn leather sole of his shoe. Instead of handing it back, he jumped down into the hole himself and started slicing away at the ropes.

Some men were working on the next tree. They had the sling technique down by now, but made room for Corvin to grab a handle before starting to lift. "One! Two!" a man shouted, another man heaved up just after "Two," and they raised the tree and its root ball, the rest rushing to keep up with the early lifter, laughing.

It was getting toward supper time, and the women were gone. There were still plenty of little kids around. Not Corvin's, though. He had expected Willy to come over by now, but he knew that Hannah wouldn't. She had never adjusted to the neighborhood and claimed that most of her Hmong classmates were in gangs. When Corvin dismissed the notion, she turned on him in anger. "What do you know?" she had shouted at him.

What did he know? Not much. These men he was working with, who joked around and laughed and squeezed his biceps when they had gotten a tree into its hole and told him, "You strong!" Were they being ironic, mocking him? Had they been soldiers, killing with knives and crossbows and automatic weapons in the mountain forests of Laos, fighting the war that had flexed its great claws at Corvin, came close, then let him get away without a scratch, let him go without even touching him? He didn't know. He didn't know much.

There were still quite a few trees left, but the job went fast now. They worked around the far side of the housing project and faced more of the wire-caged maples. Corvin went ahead and cut through the cages with his wire cutter, the only tool he had left by now, and the Hmong fathers pulled open the cages like bear traps and slung the trees into the ground with increasing abandon, measuring nothing, never stepping back to make sure the trees were straight, filling the holes without waiting for the hoses to be dragged out to the street. Every time, now, they chanted in unison, "One! Two! Three!" but nobody waited for "Three." Somebody would always strain upward suddenly on a sling handle on "Two," or before "Two," and everybody else would struggle to keep up with him so the tree wouldn't knock them backward into the dirt. It was a joke, they laughed like crazy, tired and loose after whatever bleak day they had had, enjoying the physical, communal work of planting trees.

Then they were done. The Hmong fathers lighted cigarettes, talked among themselves for a few minutes, and started heading back through the housing project. Corvin discovered that even his wire cutter was gone. He looked around in the half-light, then picked up the last DNR shovel from the boulevard and joined the others. "You from the church?" one of the men asked him as they walked. No, Corvin answered, he was just a neighbor. The man nodded. "You strong," he said.

Not many people were around when they got back to the front of the project. Nina was still helping Steve shovel forks full of mulch from the huge pile of shredded bark into a wheel barrow, but Lee and the rest of the environmental club had gone off somewhere.

At the corner, Corvin looked down one line of trees, then another. In the dim light cast by streetlamps, anyway, they looked pretty good. Steve came up and thanked him for helping. Corvin walked back with him to the DNR truck to leave the shovel, which he had been thinking about maybe keeping, to balance his losses a little. On the boulevard grass next to the truck, he found his hat, wire cutter, pruning knife, pruning shears, lopper, gloves, and shovel, all of his tools, laid out in a neat row. There was going to be mulch left over, Steve said, and told him to help himself if he needed any for his own yard. But when Corvin came back the next afternoon with his garden cart, he found that the residents had used all of it, surrounding every tree and shrub and garden in the entire housing project with neat rings of shredded bark.

The new trees survived a long, harsh winter and leafed out the following spring. The Japanese lilacs were just starting to open their first flowers when somebody came by in the night and chopped down five of them with an ax or machete that left a litter of broad, white flakes strewn over the grass like apple blossoms. Corvin's ex-wife, Rachel, was driving their kids back to his house when they discovered the damage. She told him that Hannah had started to cry,e and both children were heartbroken for him, that somebody had destroyed his hard work. He was angry and sad for a while, but after somebody came by and removed the mutilated limbs and stubbed trunks, he got over it. It was the urban forest. These things happened.

WRAPPED IN BLUE

A DREAM OF fishing. His grandfather, twelve years dead, standing unsteadily in the back of a rowboat. The boat rocking. He tries to steady it, can't, oars groping clumsily in the darkness. Sara, waking him, telling him her water has broken. It was too early. She was already dressed. It was three weeks too early.

Isaiah fumbled into his clothes and drove with his carefully breathing wife through deserted, middle-of-the-night streets to the hospital, where Sara was taken to a room different from the country-homey birthing room they had been shown on their tour, this one smaller, bleaker, with metal-framed bed and no plaid or patchwork or wicker at all, only a dark brown corduroy chair that could be opened out for the mother's partner, should things progress slowly.

Things progressed slowly. With a giant diaper installed beneath her gown for the steady hemorrhage of amniotic fluid, they walked and walked the polished corridors, but by the time the morning shift came on and the obstetrics wing started to bustle, her contractions hadn't started. The midwife came in and consulted with several doctors, and they decided it was time to start a pitocen drip to induce contractions. A nurse slid the IV needle into her arm, strapped a fetal monitor to the drum-tight dome of her belly, and plugged in the monitor recording apparatus and pitocen pump.

After about a half hour the first contraction hit her. Then nothing but ghostly aftershocks. They increased the rate of drip until finally contractions started coming at more or less regular intervals, landing abrupt as blows of a fist. Induced contractions were like that, the midwife explained, not gathering smoothly in intensity but jagged in profile, steep spikes.

These crude, manufactured contractions battered her all day. The midwife left in the afternoon, and doctors and nurses stopped by to check on her progress. Again and again strangers thrust hopeful fingers into her, yet by the evening she had progressed to only two centimeters.

Water had continued to flow from her all day, she was an inexhaustible spring. Every time the nurses stopped in, they drew the blue, absorbent paper blanket from beneath her, sopping wet, and replaced it with dry. Helping his wife get her swollen body turned and lifted a little for this blanket-changing became one of Isaiah's functions, who was otherwise mostly scared and bored, though he accepted the notion that he was serving an essential role just by being there. Nurses looked at him with approval, they were proud of him. Another function was to go to the little stainless steel pantry between the birthing room and the corridor and get ice chips for her to suck. He liked this job. The cold, sterile pantry was a refuge from the sweaty uncertainty of the birthing room, and the hopper of the icemaker was always full of fresh crushed ice.

That night they stopped the pitocen drip to give her a chance to rest, to gather her strength for the ordeal still to come. Isaiah lay fitfully on the fold-out beside her bed, unsteady dreams jolting him awake whenever he sank into sleep. Doctors periodically came into the darkened room and by flashlight examined the output of the fetal monitor, jerkily inked paper that spilled in endless accordion folds onto the floor. Once, when they were both awake, a doctor explained that after the membrane had been broken for twenty-four hours, there started to be a danger of infection.

Her voice harsh and weak from so much regimented breathing, Sara said, "Maybe we should start talking c-section."

"Well," the doctor said, "everything looks good still. We'll keep an eye on it, see how things go in the morning. Advantage of a teaching hospital, you have doctors around all night. We have a lower caesarian birth rate than any of the private hospitals."

"But if I need it."

"Sure, if you need it, no problem."

After the doctor left, Sara turned to Isaiah and made him swear he wouldn't let them make her go too long. "I might be out of it, you have to speak for me. I don't care about their god damned caesarian rate."

In the morning, they started the pitocen drip again, increasing the rate until it seemed the contractions were going to tear her apart. Still she hadn't progressed past four centimeters. She reached out and clawed for his hand and said, "This isn't working. Tell them, now."

"Sara, sweetie, when the doctor comes in, we'll talk about it." No one had been by to check on her for quite a while, any minute now somebody should be coming in.

"I can't take any more."

He went out to find a doctor. Several people ran past without ac-knowledging him, and he saw one of their doctors and some others disappearing into a room down the hall, and a nurse in intense con-versation with a young Hispanic-looking man wearing a print shirt and blue jeans. She ushered the young man into the room.

Isaiah went back in to his wife. "They're on their way," he said. She was quiet, and by the time a doctor came in she was asleep. He told the doctor what she had said. "Really," he said, "this is crazy, she's exhausted herself. You said twenty-four hours—it's been thir-ty-six. Why wait any longer?" He was trying to speak truly for her, though he knew he should be shouting, not arguing rationally. He should be grabbing the guy by the front of his scrubs and screaming in his face.

The doctor shook his head, kept staring at the endless folds of paper cascading through his hands. "No," he said, "baby's doing fine, it's strong, we'll give it a little more time." The doctor wouldn't look him in the face.

When the doctor left, she woke, and he told her what the doctor had said. She cried, "It's just pride. It's just fucking macho pride. God damn them," she kept saying. "God damn them to hell."

Isaiah knew he was included in this curse. He tried to comfort and encourage her, then retreated to the brightly lit pantry. While he was scooping ice chips into the plastic pitcher, he noticed something on the stainless steel counter, something wrapped in blue. He went over and looked at it. It was a newborn baby, sound asleep, snugly swathed in one of those absorbent paper blankets. He stared down at it. Not asleep. You don't wrap a sleeping baby in a paper blanket, leave it alone on a counter in a cold room.

He wanted to touch the baby, but he could not. He wanted to take the baby in his arms and go out into the hall and cry out and find somebody who would take care of it. Instead, he left it where it was, wrapped in blue, and took the pitcher of ice chips out the other door, into the dim and musty birthing room, and fed ice chips, one by one, between his wife's parched lips.

Finally, late in the afternoon of the second day, she started to progress, reached eight centimeters, nine. They paged the midwife. Waiting in the hall for her, Isaiah overheard some nurses talking about a c-section that had gone bad. They wheeled Sara into a blazingly lit operating room, with all the paraphernalia of IV and monitors and pitocen pump, and she was in labor for hours more. They changed to a new pump, unable to believe the rate displayed by the first one. As the night advanced, more and more hospital personnel drifted into the operating room, until the glazed tile walls were lined with women and men in festive pastels—yellow, pink, green, blue—waiting in silence.

A doctor, a white woman younger than the midwife, younger than Sara, took over, and inserted a suction device like a toilet plunger, trying to grasp the baby's head, and then put together the huge gleaming steel tongs of a forceps and jammed them somehow inside of her. "This baby got hold of a rib!" a nurse said, the only one of the six people crowded around her able to joke still. "Let go, you."

Then everything was screaming and blood and wild urging and savage, heart-felt curses and tears, and Sara drove out of herself and the doctor pulled with the fierce, enormous forceps and the midwife slid in to receive finally a slithering baby boy. And though they had planned to rush it immediately to intensive care, once they had performed the first swarming brutalities of nostril-suctioning and blood-taking and eye-swabbing, it was obvious this was a baby so strong and beautiful, they could all relax and revert to the fantastic notion that childbirth was a normal thing. The doctor sat down between Sara's splayed, trembling legs and began the long tailor's work of sewing her back together again.

When Isaiah returned the next day, he passed the young Hispanic man coming out of the maternity ward. He thought about the baby wrapped in blue. He thought about its mother, recovering in this place full of flowers and mylar balloons and the cries of living babies. He thought about the empty-handed father. Pulling on a gown of yellow paper, he followed the receptionist's direction to the room where Sara was learning to nurse their astonishing child. He kept all these things secret from her, and pondered them in his heart.

HER GOOD NAME

AFTER EIGHTEEN MONTHS in Spain, Rita Vogel returned to the United States with her ten-year-old sons, Andrew and Colin, and the body of her husband, Bruce Mehta. They flew to Minneapolis, where she buried her husband, then she found a house in the old Rondo neighborhood of St. Paul, hired a contractor, Walt Duggan, to help her renovate the American foursquare's awkward, decaying kitchen and skuzzy bathroom, and enrolled her boys in public school. She didn't stop, she didn't even slow down until she started looking for a job, and then it felt to her as if she had plowed head-on into a mountain of wet cement.

"Jesus!" She dropped the kitchen phone. There had been a crash, and heavy demolition now seemed to be going on right above her head. She ran up the stairs and tried to open the twins' bedroom door, but it pushed back, knocking her off balance. The old door rattled and quivered in its frame as the boys bashed against it, grunting with the impact of their wiry bodies pounding each other. This time she didn't bother shouting at them to stop it. She forced her way into the room, grabbed the one on top, Andrew, yanked him away and tossed him onto a bed, then put her bare foot against Colin's thin, sweaty chest and held him down till he stopped squirming and lay there panting in harsh gasps. She dragged him to his feet, and without her saying anything he headed down the hallway to her bedroom and slammed the door behind him. Andrew was sitting cross-legged on Colin's bed, breathing hard and fingering the side of his neck, exploring a long scratch that was just starting to welt and ooze blood. Rita stood there, waiting for her own heart to stop pounding. "Jesus Christ."

Bruce's insurance policy and the pension left over from his years

29

at 3M had turned out to be smaller than Rita would have guessed, had she ever thought about it, but it was not financial straits so much as the fugitive's conflicting needs to find cover and to keep moving that had set her looking for a job as soon as her explosive, mysterious sons were enrolled in school.

Before she and Bruce decided to move to Spain to pursue their old dream of starting an English language academy abroad, she had been assistant principal at two St. Paul junior high schools and one senior high. She had never loved being a public school administrator, but she had been successful at it, as successful as anybody could be who spoke her mind in a bureaucracy, and she had always assumed she could step back in if she ever wanted to. It was a big district, she wasn't picky about the school, and she would have been willing to go back into the classroom until an administrative position opened up. But there had been a lot of turn-over in the central office, and the people she dealt with now were strangers, even those she remembered from before, and she got nowhere. It didn't make sense to her.

She closed the twins' bedroom door behind her, picked up the hallway phone, and listened for a moment to the dead sound of a broken connection. It had been somebody with a thick southern accent, starting to introduce himself. She went back downstairs and hung up the kitchen phone, which she had just answered when that fraternal violence had broken loose on the second floor. Maybe it was the distraction of Andrew and Colin's violent absorption with each other that was keeping her from thinking clearly about finding a job. When they weren't fighting, they were obsessively watching television, "American television," they would always say, digging it in that she had removed them from its pleasures for a year and a half, an unnatural deprivation that had ended with the loss of their father.

They still wouldn't talk to Rita about Bruce's death and shrugged off counselors like flies. Imperceptible slights or challenges hurled them at each other, and a half hour later she would hear them singing together in eerie, tight harmony, hits from a Sounds of the Seventies TV advertisement that played fragments from the compilation CD or cassette tape while titles scrolled up the screen. That was all they knew of the songs, and they would sing those fragments one after the other, seven seconds of plaintive lyrics addressed to a beach baby at the end of summer, followed by seven seconds of mama crying in the night over dead or dying Chicago, followed by seven seconds of joy and fun in the sun. Their unchanged voices rendered the falsetto-rich love songs more perfectly than the original artists, pleas for slow and gentle rocking, followed by cryptic complaints about little Willie, who wouldn't go home, strung-together shards of a dozen songs that had trailed Rita's adolescence like actual adoring boyfriends.

But she hadn't lost her mind, and her failure to get anywhere with her job search really didn't make sense, she was enough of a professional to know that. She wondered whether her resignation and leaving the country had offended someone, had been taken as desertion by some tap-rooted old St. Paul school district bureaucrat now invisibly undercutting her no matter whom she approached. That was the scenario she had recently laid out for Walt, who had become her lover sometime between the installation of a pedestal sink in the bathroom and the sanding of her kitchen floor. She hadn't said anything about it to her brother, Tom, with whom she had once been very close, or to her friends, the few friends with whom she had had time to reconnect. She really hadn't reconnected with anyone beyond having lunch or coffee, giving someone an awkward tour of her new old house, promising to get together again soon. Rita didn't have the heart for it, and nobody except Walt had been willing to push past the grim edges of her privacy. She hadn't talked with Tom in months.

Before she had a chance to go upstairs and see if her boys had cooled off, the phone rang again. "We must have gotten cut off," the caller said, who introduced himself as a reporter from the *Dallas Morning News*. He said he was calling to ask her for a statement about a court ruling. She didn't know what he was talking about, and he paused, and then said, with deliberate patience, "The ruling relieving the Church of Christ Scientist of responsibility in the death of your son."

She hung up on him, thinking it was a crank call. That evening, after a local television station called with essentially the same question, she told Walt about it. He was finishing the baseboard molding in the bathroom, and she sat on the closed toilet seat while he squeezed himself into position to drive home a finishing nail with his power nailer. The air in the bathroom was heavy with turpentine from the pine wainscoting she had stained and varnished a few days before, vinyl fumes from a shower curtain still creased from the package, and the tobacco smoke that clung to Walt's giant overalls like another layer of fabric. Good smells, but they were making her feel lightheaded.

Walt held the nail gun in place for a moment without firing, then drew himself up into a kneeling position on the black and white checkerboard tiles, a big man who pretty much filled the open space between the tub and the toilet. "I wondered about that," he said, and seemed to study her face, looking for what? "It's the coincidence of your name," he said. "When you called about the renovation and left your name for me, I thought...." He had dense gray hair that stood up like the fur on a malamute, begging to be petted. The first time they had touched, it had been her palm grazing across that strange softness.

Now she kept her hands folded between her knees. "Thought what?" A sense of someone's secret knowledge pressed in between them.

He made little clicking noises with a switch on the power nailer until she reached over and tried to take it out of his hands, and he set the heavy tool down on the tiles. He said, "Year, year and a half ago there was this trial in Minneapolis, a Christian Science woman's son died from diabetes. She refused medical treatment for him. They acquitted her, then her ex-husband—the kid's father—sues her and her new husband and the Christian Science church, I don't know who else. Her name's Rita Vogel." He looked at her but didn't quite meet her eyes. "When I got your message on my answering machine, I thought you were her."

The room was tilting, and Rita shifted her feet to brace against it. "When did you figure it out, Walt?" It came out sounding harsh and sarcastic. The smells in the tiny room were making her sick.

"Soon as we met, I knew you were a different Rita Vogel. I'd seen her on TV. Turns out, she's living with her new husband in Oregon now, the other Rita Vogel. I've been sort of following it. Vogel's her second husband's name. The kid had a different last name."

He stopped, listening. She heard it too, sugary, drawn-out insistence that it was ma-gic, Andrew and Colin singing in their bedroom down the hall. Rumors of Shannon, gone, floating out to sea.

This was the conspiracy, she thought, this was it, keeping this stupid coincidence from her. Since Bruce's death and her return from Spain, she hadn't paid attention to the news, she had been absorbed in trying to take care of her boys' needs, fixing up the house, negotiating the relationship with Walt, looking for a job. Threading her way through the swamp of grief, avoiding its quicksand, had taken every remaining bit of her attention. Still, she couldn't believe she hadn't known about something so intimately touching her, smearing religious fanaticism over her good name. Somebody would have talked to her about it. A dozen people would have. Her mind's gaze began darting around, searching conversations that maybe had, in fact, had that subtext.

"You were out of the country when the whole thing happened."

"It was on television?"

"I thought you knew about it. Now there's this lawsuit from the natural father. Five and a half million dollars."

"It's unbelievable. It's just unbelievable."

"It has nothing to do with you."

"Nothing except my goddamn name. Nothing except that everybody in the country from here to Dallas thinks I'm that faith-healing child killer."

"It didn't seem to be that big a story, once the criminal trial was over. I'm surprised the Texas paper picked up on it now."

She looked past Walt's big, kind face, studied the interrupted grain of the wainscoting. "This is why they won't hire me," she said.

"It crossed my mind. But they've got to know it wasn't you. She's living in Oregon."

"Crossed your mind? No, this is why. This is why." The fumy little room turned and turned underneath her, but there was a gravity holding her now that had nothing to do with the earth, and she felt herself revolve around its center, as helplessly obedient to its pull as a swung pail of water.

She was still in the grip of this stunned certainty the following day when she hesitantly answered the phone in the upstairs hall. This time it was her mother's voice, thin and crackly. "Darling, give me the directions to your house, we don't even know where you and the boys live since you moved from that awful apartment, I'm still furious with your father for dragging me off to Israel when I knew you needed me here."

When Bruce died, eight months before, Rita's parents, Joanna and Doug, had been about to leave on a tour of the Holy Land that Doug's congregation had given them as a retirement bonus. They had delayed it to attend the funeral, but the window was about to close on the trip, and Rita had insisted they go ahead, she had plenty of support from her friends and her brother Tom, who lived only a few hours away, though in fact at the time she had just wanted to be by herself as much as possible. Back from the tour, her parents had had to close on their new house in North Carolina and then deal with its remodeling, and after that Rita had dodged their suggestions of a visit like thrown axes. She had put them off with a vague promise that, yes, they maybe could go on vacation together sometime, a road trip like when she was a kid. When she was growing up, those vacations were the only times the family had had to themselves, away from congregation and church committees and community organizations, her mother as busy as her father. In Rita's memory, the world seen through their station wagon windows was more welcoming, somehow, than their own living room. Rancorous as they often were, the trips carried a nostalgic aura of closeness for all of them, and over the years somebody or other would periodically suggest resurrecting them. It had seemed like a safe thing to mention.

"You're coming up?"

"We're here, kid, surprise! Only your father's gotten us lost."

While Rita tried to explain the maze of sewer separation street work that was blockading her part of the city, she heard the doorbell ring downstairs and somebody rattling the screen door. She called down to Walt to get it. He was in the kitchen, installing a garbage disposal, and she heard him say something to whomever it was at the front door, and then her mother over the cell phone shouting away from the mouthpiece, "Doug, for God's sake, would you wait a minute, she's telling me!" And then her father's voice from downstairs, shouting, "This is it! I told you! Get off the phone and come in!" and her mother over the phone again, shouting to him, "I'm sure she said blue! This is clearly gray!" And then to Rita, "Dear, you don't live in a gray house, do you? Your father—" The connection broke and Rita heard her father's booming preacher's voice downstairs introducing himself to Walt and hollering up to her about getting him a drink.

That evening, at supper, everybody seemed to get along, though Joanna was obviously hurt that she hadn't heard about Walt before, and must have been disconcerted to find a stranger in what she would have regarded as Bruce's place. Joanna and Doug had adored Bruce. Rita had expected them to oppose her marriage to a man of color, a Hindu by descent though a Presbyterian in practice, but they had taken to him from the start. She had always regarded her parents as conservative to the point of bigotry, and despite her relief, it had burned her a little, their obvious gratitude that somebody so stable and accomplished had chosen to marry her. And of course they loved him for giving them grandchildren, such dark, handsome boys, they would always say.

When Joanna announced her plan now—for all of them to drive out to the Black Hills—she was vague about whether or not Walt was to be included. He made it easy for her, explaining without being asked that he was in the middle of a townhouse renovation in

Minneapolis that was behind schedule. Joanna had brought along a tourist guide to the western United States. She opened it at the table and went through a pink-highlighted itinerary—Corn Palace, the Badlands, Wall Drug, Crazy Horse memorial, Mt. Rushmore, Hot Springs, Jewel Cave, Little Bighorn battlefield, Yellowstone, Grand Tetons—going on as if they would be traveling together all summer.

Andrew interrupted her. "We got baseball," he said. "We can't miss our games. In Little League you aren't even supposed to miss practice."

The boys were seated between Doug and Joanna. Colin turned to his grandfather and said, "He's worried about being cut. He hasn't got a hit in three games," and almost before the words were out of his mouth Andrew hurled himself onto him. The chair went over backward and crashed into a sideboard and the tangled boys bashed at each other with their fists and knees and feet. After a moment's shock, Doug and Joanna staggered up and grabbed at them, trying to drag them apart. They didn't know how to get a good grip on them, however, the whirl of limbs was too furious, and Rita couldn't reach them, her parents were in the way. She watched over her father's struggling shoulders, the boys' straight black hair flying into wild mops as they banged against table and chair legs and their heads struck the wooden floor and the thrashing of their bodies sent glasses crashing onto plates and silverware flying and a wild screaming.

Rita stared helplessly. It looked like a boy fighting himself. She had to do something. She had to get the boys out of this house for a while, which they had never known as anything but a work in progress. Any change would be a change for the better, even if only for a few days.

After they finally separated the twins and sent them to opposite ends of the house, Rita realized that the screaming had been Joanna. She had never seen her mother in such hysteria, her aristocratic face blotchy with dismay. Walt cleaned up the mess while Rita went to talk to the boys and Doug took Joanna out for a cigarette and a calming drive. He needed to get to a liquor store, anyway.

An hour later, Joanna was sitting on the couch in the living room between the boys, balancing a glass on one knee and showing them pictures from the Holy Land tour, page after page of photos sealed in mylar pockets, three fat albums she had probably started organizing the day the film was developed. The envelopes of photos Rita had sporadically taken while she and Bruce were traveling around Spain looking for a suitable location for their language school were lost somewhere in a cardboard box, in the attic or basement or the double garage Walt had built for her, jammed in with cartons of old toys and books and clothes and housewares she had left in rented storage in Minneapolis when they sold their house and went abroad. She could get physically sick thinking about all that crap, and she sometimes thought it would be worth while to have everything burn to the ground, just so she wouldn't have to sort through it, ever. Bruce's clothes were in some of those boxes. His fountain pen collection. His chemistry textbooks from college and his framed engineering diploma and every card and letter she had ever written him.

Walt was bending over a road map spread out on the cleared dining room table, pointing out vaguely remembered road conditions and attractions to Doug, who stood there with a scotch in his hand. Her father's hair was whiter than Rita remembered it, maybe because he was so darkly tanned now, the back of his neck burned nearly oxblood above the collar of his expensive golf shirt. Doug was pretending to be interested in what Walt was saying, but he was probably thinking about something completely different—what a deal he had gotten on his new minivan, or something he had seen in Bethlehem that would have made a wonderful point in a sermon, or maybe wondering how this enormous blue-collar worker had somehow replaced his soft-spoken, refined, comfortably exotic son-in-law. At fifty-seven, Walt was half way between Rita and her parents in age. It would have been unbearably strange to travel with all of them together, the sweet simplification of a road trip tangled between her abandoned past and her incomprehensible future.

Joanna joined them, surveying the Post-it notes in her AAA tour guide. "This mammoth site in Hot Springs sounds fascinating," she said. "When we were in Israel, I decided that that was what I wanted to do with the rest of my life." She looked around the room, waiting. "Archaeology," she explained, when nobody said anything. "Hiking around in all those wonderful excavations, I kept thinking about Bruce, that he would have been the one to understand what it meant to me."

Why? Rita wanted to ask her. Why would he have understood, more than the rest of them? And then she had to admit to herself that he would have. He always understood other people's passions. He deferred to them, honoring what he himself somehow lacked. He would have hurled himself enthusiastically into the trip and made everyone's enjoyment of it that much richer. The school in Spain hadn't been their old dream, it was her old dream, since her junior year abroad. He had made it happen.

Rita resolved to make the best of the present situation. She called the boys' coach at home that evening, and he said it would be okay if they missed a week or so, everybody went on vacation. She tried to think of it that way, a vacation, rather than shock therapy. It would be good to escape from the telephone, anyway. Her stomach turned every time it rang, as if reporters were actively hunting her down, hungry for her murderous scoop, though in fact there had been no more calls from them.

Doug and Joanna had made arrangements with Rita's brother to go on the trip before they had sprung the plan on her. The day after their arrival, Tom drove down from Duluth, and the next morning they set out in two cars, Doug's Aerostar van and Tom's little Geo. Doug wanted them all to go in the van, but by the time they started packing up, the twins had demonstrated to everyone's satisfaction that they wouldn't survive twelve hundred miles trapped together in even the spacious luxury of the loaded Aerostar.

Rita started out with Tom and Andrew. Doug drove eighty, eighty-five miles per hour on the interstate, and Tom struggled to keep him in sight. Rita could see the tension in Tom's face when the

Aerostar disappeared around a sweeping turn or when a few vehicles separated them. At forty-two years old, Tom was starting to look like his father. His hair was a blond that had never been far from white, and his hairline had risen into the same high, ecclesiastical arch. His jaw was filling out, he was getting that little pot. If he traded his tiny, wire-rim oval glasses for Doug's fishbowl aviators, the resemblance would have been creepy. It was creepy anyway.

They stopped every hour or two to let the boys trade cars, and sometimes Joanna rode with Tom and Rita rode with her father. When she was in the Aerostar, Rita never said anything to her father about maybe slowing down, or that Tom was worried he would go sailing past them, unaware, when the van had pulled over at a rest stop some time. On the last stretch of highway before Mitchell, South Dakota, the boys decided to ride together with Tom, and Rita rode with her mother and father, who talked constantly in their stereo fashion about their Holy Land trip and their new home outside of Asheville and the boys and what Tom and Rita had been like at their age and Tom's new job in Duluth. They avoided the subject of Walt. Rita was irritated by this, but she also dreaded trying to explain a relationship she didn't understand herself, just needed, felt grateful for. Rita noticed that Joanna was studying her in the vanity mirror she had adjusted for this purpose. "What?"

"I have to ask you," Joanna said. "The other night at supper— what's wrong with those poor boys? They were like animals." Rita knew what it meant for her mother to acknowledge flaws in her only grandchildren, and she resisted the urge to lash out in wounded defense of them.

"It's been hard for them," she said. "They've lost their father."

"Of course it's hard, there's been so many changes and everything is upside down. But I never saw anything like that. You and Tom had squabbles, but nothing like that."

"It's different with twins, everything is more intense. They're getting better," Rita said. As she said it, she realized that her mother was not criticizing the boys, she was criticizing her. For leaving the country. For managing to lose Bruce. For having another man in her life already, someone so different from what they would have imagined. She felt the list ravel on. For not having a church. (That was one of her father's first questions—where would they go to church the next morning, which Rita hadn't even remembered was Sunday.) Her own, self-blame list was long enough, she had no trouble filling in theirs. For raising her boys in the inner city, which probably seemed to her parents like one more dangerous foreign country. ("Is this neighborhood all blacks and Orientals?" she had asked Rita when they were sitting on the front porch the previous evening, watching neighbors walk by.) For not having a job. For…. Really, it could go on forever.

Rita sank back in the plush middle seat of the van and pretended to doze, feeling the land sway and tremble underneath her. When they got to Mitchell, she waited at the sun-blasted curb outside the Corn Palace to let Tom know where the van was parked. He drove up with the boys hanging out of the little car's windows like dogs.

"We're fried!" Andrew screamed at her, and when they were all together in the cool mustiness of the Corn Palace lobby, Tom told her that the Geo's air conditioner had stopped working. The boys' hair was blown into wild tangles that Joanna set to work on with comb and brush from her purse. Wind-blown, Tom looked like a heavier Art Garfunkel. Not a bad look, Rita thought, but he disappeared into a restroom and returned with the frizz damp and subjugated, his still-red face a few degrees closer to normal.

Doug handed Tom one of his business cards, on the back of which he had written the name and address of a Chevy dealer in Mitchell where Tom could get the a/c looked at. He had made inquiries among Corn Palace employees while Tom was in the restroom, and they had told him this was the place to go.

First, though, they had to tour the Corn Palace. Tourist attractions had always been pilgrimage shrines to the Vogels. Nobody questioned the obligation to do homage at them, particularly if it was a AAA starred attraction, as the Corn Palace certainly was. It was actually just a sort of auditorium, Rita discovered, with display cases of Indian and pioneer artifacts and blown-up photographs of fantastic Corn Palaces from the turn of the century, the building covered with intricate mosaics created with ears of corn and other harvest vegetation. Now, in the middle of summer, it was just concrete and painted depictions of corn.

Every once in a while, Rita could hear Andrew and Colin screaming somewhere in the cavernous space, their high voices ringing off the walls in what might have been either delight or anger. Relaxing into a stupor of dutiful studiousness, she lost track of them as she wandered from display to display, studying the old photographs, examining the artifacts. If Bruce had been there, he would have been reading the captions aloud to her. She read one label herself, hearing his voice. It explained an atlatl, a spearthrower from before the invention of the bow and arrow. In a faded painting, hunters were using atlatls to hurl toothpick spears into a gigantic wooly mammoth. In the next display case there were little piles of ancient withered seeds arranged behind the glass. Somebody had painstakingly gathered them. Somebody's family had gone hungry because they had been misplaced.

Rita wandered out finally into the furious blast of sun and found the others across the street at a little souvenir mall, having ice cream. There was a stuffed effigy of an Indian chief propped on a bench, where you could have your picture taken sitting beside it, and her sons were there on the bench, eating ice cream cones. She hoped nobody had taken their picture with the effigy, then saw her mother snapping away and her father with his video camera capturing it for all time. She offered to go to the Chevy place with Tom, but Colin started screwing around with the chief's feather headdress, trying to take it off, and she decided to go with her parents and the boys to an Indian archaeological site just outside of town. She wanted them to see at least one thing authentic on the trip, not just effigies and painted concrete corncobs and the heads of presidents blasted into a mountain.

A stream separated the parking lot from the archaeological site's interpretive center, crossed by a suspended wooden bridge. Colin raced ahead and whooped as the bridge swayed beneath him, then he and Andrew ran back and forth on it until it was swinging wildly. Rita reached the bridge before her parents and told the boys to knock it off, but as she crossed it herself and felt it sway uncontrollably beneath her, she decided that it was meant to do this, to be entertainingly unstable. It felt like being drunk. Joanna shrieked and clung to the side ropes as she crossed, and Doug had the idea of filming the scene ahead of him as he wobbled across. Rita had never seen either of her parents actually drunk, staggering drunk, but it seemed to her that they drank a lot, for a Lutheran minister and his wife. She herself had crossed the bridge as quickly as she could, holding her breath.

In the low-slung, sprawling interpretive center there were life-size dioramas of prehistoric dwellings, dome-shaped huts made out of branches and clean-smelling bark, stone and wood implements, and a stuffed buffalo. Rita hurried her parents and sons through it, hungry for contact with the actual dwellings, the hollowed earth that had sheltered families thousands of years before the European invasion. A teenage girl sold them tickets and a teenage boy gave them a brief, canned lecture on the pre-Mandan builders of the village they were about to visit, before sending them out for the self-guided tour, armed with brochures and a site map.

It looked like pasture, a fifteen-or-twenty-acre field of comfortably low rolling hills. Rita kept her parents and the twins together at first, trying to follow the paths from site to site that were marked on the map, but it seemed impossible to relate the map to what they were actually seeing—faint traces of footsteps in the dry, beaten grass, scattered posts topped with plastic-laminated, unilluminating text. There were stone outcroppings here and there that always looked promising from a distance, but each of them turned out to be nothing but unshaped, random rocks rather than the excavations they were looking for.

Soon the boys were racing to the far limits of the field, in and out of sight among the hills. Rita searched for the diggings, the post-holes and low walls and bone middens pictured in the brochure. She crisscrossed the field under the brutal sun until she noticed that even the boys had given up and were walking with their grandparents back up the hill to the shady tables near the interpretive center. She kept looking, stopping only to study the map, turning with it to orient herself by the obscure landmarks, then striding off again, certain every time she spotted a new marker that she had broken the code, that she would be able to shout up to the others and wave her arms and lead them back to her discovery. "There," she would say. "There. That's what we came to see."

Sweaty, sunburned, eventually she gave up, too, and trudged up the hill feeling stupid and blind. When they all went back inside and confessed their failure, the teenage boy explained that a couple of years ago they had filled in all of the excavations, having discovered that the weather was quickly eroding artifacts that the earth had protected for thousands of years. He showed them an architect's drawing of something he referred to as an archeodome, which he said they were going to build someday, a great glass bubble that would shelter the diggings, and pointed out a jar half-filled with dollar bills, donations for the archeodome. Doug told the boy he thought they should refund the five dollars admission each adult had paid to see the excavated village, but then Andrew reported that Tom had arrived, and the boys ran down to meet him. All the way down to the bridge, which Andrew and Colin had swinging and creaking in an ecstasy of instability, Rita listened to Doug and Joanna complain about the fraud, until she had to ask them to just shut up about it. They looked at each other in hurt surprise.

They didn't get to Chamberlain, where they had motel reservations, until almost eight o'clock in the evening. Doug came out of the motel office with an expression of grim satisfaction on his face.

"What?" Rita asked him as he distributed their room keys.

"That woman in there, when I gave her my name, she told me, 'I cancelled you out, Buddy. You were supposed to be here by six.' She wanted me to be scared, and then she expected me to be grateful that she'd still manage to find us rooms, which any fool would know after one look at this parking lot wasn't going to be a problem." Joanna started to rag on him for not calling ahead when they knew they were behind schedule, but he just rolled on with his story and after a few overlapping sentences she gave up. "I made her an offer," he said. "I said, 'We'll stay here if we get the AARP discount,' and she said, 'Okay,' as if she had a choice, and I said to her, 'All of us. All of us get the AARP discount, or the six of us keep right on going and you can sit on those empty rooms tonight.'" None of them had to ask him if they had gotten the retired persons' discounts, including the ten year olds, and Tom, and Rita, not yet forty. "You better believe we got them," he said finally. "'Buddy.'"

After they had gotten settled, Rita and Tom went for a walk down to the river and the long, steel-framed bridge over the Missouri that starts in the Midwest and ends in the West, a purple spill of bluffs that spread into the evening.

"It made his day," Tom said, leaning over the swirling water halfway across the bridge. "You've got to admire him. The guy knows how to get his way."

"How's it going for you these days, Tom?" Rita felt guilty that she didn't return his calls more faithfully, that she resorted to blaming the boys for not letting her know when he left messages. They had been close when they were kids, but after Tom went to the seminary, Rita had had a falling out with him for trying to be a little copy of Doug, and for not asserting the fact of his gayness, which they had held from their parents as a restless secret throughout high school. When he had come out to Joanna and Doug after ordination, Rita felt they just pretended to accept it, competing with each other for who was most tolerant, when she knew it must have just about killed them both that their perfect child, the one who earned perfect grades, never got into trouble, dutifully followed his father's dreams, that he was the one who had harbored this shock for them. She wondered if they had somehow diverted the blame to her, for not telling them.

Tom was the assistant director of a social service agency in Duluth now, a ministry for street people, alcoholics, drug addicts, runaways. "I couldn't be prouder of him," Joanna had said to Rita in the van earlier that day.

"He's inspiring," Doug had said. "My ministry pales in comparison with his devotion to those people." It had sounded to Rita like something he had written, and she would have given odds that he had, in some letter to the editor or some sermon. Probably both. Judging from how they talked about it, they accepted Tom's sexual orientation as a cross, a divine burden laid on them as well as on Tom. It didn't seem to have occurred to them that Tom might be having, in fact, a pretty good time now that he was out of the closet.

"What's the scene like up there?" Rita asked. "Duluth."

"You wouldn't call it a scene," he said. "Bit of stage business. A few lines of dialogue."

She looked at him, standing with a Teva-sandaled foot thrust into the bridge's ironwork, relaxed and handsome, and wished she had gone with him to get his a/c fixed instead of tramping after ghosts in the musty Corn Palace and scorching archeological site.

"There's a couple bars. A community. It's not as bad as you'd think. Though I'm thinking of moving back to the Cities."

She waited for him to talk about it, wondering whether he was in a relationship, but after the arguments of the last few years, she didn't feel she had a right to ask.

"You?"

She shrugged, started out toward the far shore, but the bridge seemed to go on forever and she felt suddenly lonely and returned to the little outlook ledge in the middle where Tom was still standing.

"It must be brutal," he said.

She laughed, the sound dry and crooked in her throat. "You don't know the half of it," she said. She didn't know where to start, how Bruce's death had torn the ground from underneath her feet, sent her scrambling for some solid place where she could catch her breath, how Walt had just appeared, a safe, good man, she thought, then found she had fallen in love with him, when the last thing she had wanted was any more falling of any kind. She had no words for any of this, and instead told Tom about the reporters' calls, the other Rita Vogel, her trouble finding a job because of the confusion—an interesting story of mistaken identity, she thought, however sickening to her. He listened quietly. As her story wound down, she looked at him. "You knew about it already," she said.

"Not about the job thing, about the other Rita Vogel."

"Did everybody know about this but me?"

"It was in the news, Rita."

"Christ. Jesus Christ."

"Actually, Mom wrote me about it when you were in Spain, and then I started paying attention. She heard about the new court case on the radio when they were out for a drive last week and called me up. She loves that car telephone." Rita stared down at the flint-gray water. "She was worried about you," Tom said.

"That's why we're on this stupid trip?"

"It's just bad luck, the name thing. She told me not to bring it up, I think it just got her thinking about you, and she had to see you and the boys. You didn't let any of us do much for you after Bruce died."

"Well, I'm really sorry, Tom. Wouldn't you know I'd be a failure as a bereaved widow, too? Wouldn't you fucking know I'd blow that, too?"

"Come on."

"Maybe it really was me, that stupid religious fanatic. Maybe I did let my kid die, too, not just my husband."

"Come on, Rita, that's not fair."

She turned and walked away, her feet ringing a little on the metal grid of the bridge's walkway. When she realized that she was heading west again, toward the darkness of those hills, the sun nothing but a pale glow in the sky beyond them, she couldn't stop. She was furious and relieved when Tom caught up with her and grabbed her by the arm and stopped her.

"We just want to help. What's so awful about that?"

She didn't know what was so awful about it. Only that it was. But she walked back with him, letting him hold her hand awkwardly on the narrow walkway. They found a bar that specialized in deep fried pieces of steak, which they ordered out of curiosity and let congeal on a plate between them while they drank a few beers, and she tried to tell him about Walt, and he tried to tell her about loving the Lord and not being able to stop thinking about this real estate broker from Minneapolis he had met the week before.

As they drove through the rolling landscape of the new West the next morning, Joanna brought up the unfortunate name coincidence as if had been a matter of open discussion all along. "I thought of writing you about it when you were abroad," she said, "but, well, I had the impression you weren't interested in news from home."

"That's ridiculous." Rita was sitting directly behind Joanna and they made eye contact only in the vanity mirror. Doug wasn't saying much, eyes behind reflective trooper sunglasses fixed on the road ahead. Rita suspected that he was a little hung over from cocktails he and Joanna had been drinking in their room when she and Tom returned from the bar the night before. Now Andrew was lying down in the third seat, stretched out with a seat belt loosely draped across his middle, earphones from his Walkman clamped across his head. His eyes were closed, though not in sleep. When he slept, he always slept on his stomach.

Joanna said, "I can't help thinking that it wouldn't have been an issue if you'd just taken Bruce's name when you married."

"Don't you think that would have been confusing, Mom, both of us being called Bruce?" Doug made a noise that might have been a cough of disapproval or might have been a laugh, and Joanna slapped the vanity mirror closed against the ceiling. What would they say if she told them the truth, that it hadn't been feminist principles that kept her from becoming Rita Mehta, it was just the silly sound of it? Actually, they would probably have had more sympathy for that, but it was too late now.

She stared out the window at the slow rotation of dull, yellow-green prairie away from them. It was true, what Joanna had said about news from home. Although she had promised everyone that she would write regularly, she soon had found herself sending nothing but xeroxed generic narratives of their experiences in Valladolid, and after a few months even these had degenerated into vague greetings tacked onto Bruce's long, charming letters. She didn't know what was wrong with her, but her anonymity in the old industrial city with its medieval core enthralled her somehow, and although she let people back home believe that she was becoming integrated with their new Spanish friends, in fact she had just pulled her husband and sons closer and closer to her. Setting up the school and then running its little classes filled every inch of available space. Red tape marked her boundaries, the life in their modern, cramped apartment was all the life she cared about anymore. She had never felt so feverishly happy. When Bruce died, it was not as if she had lost someone. It was as if a guided missile had homed in on her, exploded everything, leaving her and her sons staggering naked into a world of rubble. It wasn't even about Bruce, she was the target. That's how it had seemed to her, and it seemed that way still, however insane it would have sounded if she ever admitted it to anyone.

She felt the van swerve a little and heard her father grunt in surprise, slowing down as Tom's Geo wavered past, Tom staring straight ahead, white-faced with the unaccustomed speed he had had to muster to catch up with Doug, and Colin mouthing something through the passenger window and waving his arms.

Andrew was up, waving back to him. "He wants us to stop, Grandpa," Andrew shouted. "We missed the Badlands!"

"We'll catch them on the way back," Doug said. "I'd like to get to Wall by lunchtime."

"Colin wants to stop! Colin wants to stop!"

"*You* stop!" Rita ordered, but Andrew was out of control and didn't calm down until they turned off at an overpass exit and pulled over onto the shoulder of a deserted road that intersected the freeway, making a straight line between south and north nowhere. Tom pulled up behind them (he had dropped back after getting his father's attention), got out, and walked up for a consultation. Colin leaped out of the Geo and ran ahead of him.

Doug was irritated. Joanna made a show of chiding him for his impatience, though it was clear she thought knuckling under to the twins' selfish desires was just contributing to their maladjustment. Bruce had always managed an easy discipline with the boys. They all finally agreed to go back to Cactus Flats and take the Badlands loop without spending too much time sightseeing, so they could still make it to Wall in the early afternoon. The boys rode together in the van. Rita rode with Tom.

On the map it didn't look much longer, and they roared determinedly past an elaborate Prairie Homestead site that Rita thought they should see, but then the van started slowing ahead of them at scenic overlooks, which grew more and more spectacular, gorges dramatically eroded into the prairie. Only a few miles into the Badlands loop, they came upon a formation that rose out of the desert like a fantasy castle, a jagged miniature mountain range with peaks impossibly vertical, spires piled above spires, and it probably didn't take much screaming on the boys' part to get their grandfather to pull into a parking area across the road from it. Doug and Joanna got out but stayed close to the van, Doug panning the scene with his camcorder. Through her father's binoculars, Rita saw climbers moving high among the jagged peaks, adults and kids working their way along invisible ledges. The boys had run ahead, and Rita and Tom followed them, shading their eyes from the glare of sun off the yellow stone, edges of the world broken jaggedly, streaked with pink and brown against the hard blue sky, and watched the boys scramble up paths carved into the base of the formation's steep, fissured walls. There were some other kids climbing, and a few adults, and Andrew and Colin kept moving away from them, scrambling on all fours like monkeys and boosting themselves up onto higher and more distant ledges as the formation swung away from the highway into the open prairie.

Rita called out to them to be careful, to not go up too high, and

when they ignored her she handed the binoculars to Tom and started up after them. "I'll do it," Tom shouted when she was maybe
twenty feet up, but she had committed herself, and it felt good to
stretch her car-cramped limbs. It was easy climbing at first, where
the soft stone and compressed sand and clay and ash had been worn
into something like steps, then more difficult, the paths branching
and switching back confusingly until she found that she couldn't
see the boys anymore. Although she was maybe only a hundred feet
above the prairie floor, she felt queasy and shouted down to Tom to
call the boys back. She clung to the cool, crumbly edge of a crevice
in the rock wall as Tom walked along the base of the formation and
apparently spotted them somewhere around a turn and shouted up
at them until finally Andrew appeared, on a ledge ten or fifteen feet
below her. Andrew heard her calling to him and waved, then made
his way down to the next level, sliding, letting himself drop from
level to level.

Rita reached the ground about the same time he did, and then
the two of them joined Tom in shouting directions up to Colin,
who was slowly making his way along a much higher ridge and kept
looking up at the rocks jutting into space behind him. He was shouting something down to them.

"He wants to go all the way to the top," Andrew said. Rita and
Tom cupped their hands into megaphones and shouted no, he had
to come back down, now, right now, come back down right now,
their grandparents wanted to leave. Tom offered to go up and get
him, but then Colin apparently gave in and made his way without
further fuss down a long incline that Rita thought she had used to
get up but hadn't been able to find on her way down.

Colin was angry when he reached the ground, and Andrew
joined him in complaining about having had the first fun they had
experienced on the trip cruelly cut short. They complained the rest
of the way through the Badlands loop, seeing nothing that was interesting to them, even when there were buffalo in the distance, even
when the road started to wind upward at the western end of the loop

and the vistas grew longer and more varied. "We've got to climb that mountain again," they kept insisting from the back seat of the little car, and Rita finally said that they might be able to on the way back. Tom gave her a look and nodded at the minivan taking a switchback a few hundred feet above them. The climbing road was making her feel lightheaded, though the terrain here was not particularly dramatic. "Well," she said, "maybe we can. But we're going to see a lot of wonderful things in the next few days."

"Nothing's going to be as good as that mountain," Colin insisted.

And as far as the boys were concerned, in their five days of sightseeing in the Black Hills, nothing was. Not the weirdly flowing stone accretions inside Jewel Cave, where they hiked along aluminum walkways, the chemicals of their breath invisibly etching the earth's cold darkness, nor the distant irrelevancy of Mt. Rushmore's presidential heads, nor certainly the Crazy Horse monument, which they glimpsed from the start of the road beyond which you have to pay admission to go, a barely discernible figment of somebody's imagination. Not even the mammoth site in Hot Springs was as good, according to them, though it was paleontology's wet dream, a real archeodome actually in place here, and many lifetimes of discovery crammed into a perfect stone bowl maybe two hundred feet across, where animals had blundered into eternity eons ago, centuries of bull mammoths who could figure nothing better to do than slide down into the ancient muddy sinkhole and drown or starve to death there, leaving a forest of their bones like the ribs of shipwrecks thrusting out of the golden stone, and a walkway circled around it, with earphones telling every visitor exactly what was what.

Not even Wall Drug was as good, where a pharmacy souvenir stand had sprawled and spread to Jurassic proportions, swallowing a town whole and offering to the visitor every piece of Indian and cowboy and pioneer and wildlife and mineral gimcrackery that had ever seduced a ten-year-old boy. Wall had seduced Joanna, though, who wanted on their return trip to roam one more time the aisles of its pretend streets in search of the Black Hills Gold jewelry that so unaccountably appealed to her. But it was a place thoroughly resistible to Andrew and Colin, who wanted only to go as quickly as possible back to their own discovery, burnished now by five days' separation, that geological formation that was too perfect to be a miniature of anything, it was simply what every mountain would be in a perfect world, fitting them perfectly.

In Wall, the twins ground everyone's patience down to the raw nerve. Sarsaparilla tasted like piss, they announced repeatedly. Colin refused to sit on a shady bench outside the stores where the adults were trying to shop or have a cold drink, and Andrew kept running in screaming that his brother was standing out in the middle of the street. They had all been together too long to let it go, and even Tom, who never lost his temper, grabbed Andrew by the shoulder and marched him outside and shouted at Colin to come over and sit down, it wasn't funny anymore.

Finally Rita left Doug and Joanna and Tom in Wall and drove the boys in Tom's Geo on the interstate straight back to Cactus Flats and the eastern beginning of the Badlands loop, where the others would join them at the matchless formation in an hour or two. "Climb your butts off, boys," Doug had said to them, then went back into the Old West saloon where he and Tom were going to have another drink and wait for the jewelry-prospecting Joanna.

When Rita and the twins reached the formation and got out of the car, the heat of the afternoon sun pushed down on her like a huge hand. There were fewer cars in the parking area than when they had visited the first time, and fewer climbers on the jutting mass of yellow stone. Colin was just a patch of white T-shirt and shorts high above her by the time Rita had climbed to the first, easy paths. She couldn't see Andrew at all, and she panicked for a moment, searching the fissured stone mass for his red shirt and khaki shorts, then met him as he made his way around a turn of the cliff, heading back toward her. He was crying.

"What's the matter?" she asked.

He shrugged, keeping both hands on the rock wall. "That bastard."

"What'd he do? Did he hurt you?"

"He didn't do anything to me!" Andrew screamed at her, so violently he almost lost his balance on the ledge and knocked his baseball cap off clutching himself closer to the side of the formation. Rita eased forward and cautiously retrieved it for him, the Little League Giants cap the boys wore all summer.

"Okay, sweetie," she said. "You want a hand getting down?"

"I'm fine," he said, but followed her the fifty or sixty feet they still had to negotiate to zigzag down to the prairie floor. "This climbing thing is actually mostly Colin's deal," he admitted to her when they were on the ground. He looked up, squeezing the bill of his cap into a tube against the sun. "I can't see him anymore."

Neither could Rita. She walked along the base of the formation, peering up into the glare off the mass of cracked, eroded, tawny stone. She started shouting his name, just needing to know where he was, at first, then shouting for him to come down. It was as if he had disappeared into the towers of stone.

Andrew ran ahead of her, peering up, and suddenly screamed, "I see him! He's going to make it! He's going to make it to the top this time!"

Rita had to crouch down next to Andrew to follow the line of his skinny, outstretched arm and hand and finger to where he was pointing, and even then it was a while before she spotted the speck of white that at first she refused to believe was her son, he was so high, motionless at the base of an enormous boulder blocking a notch between pinnacles thrust into the blue-white sky. Then the speck moved a little, edging around the side of the boulder, and she knew it was Colin.

This time she didn't even try shouting—there was no possibility of her voice rising to that height. "What's he doing?" she asked Andrew. "Is he trying to get down? Do you think he's in trouble?"

"He's not in trouble," Andrew said, but there was uncertainty in his voice. "He's just got to go a little higher up and he'll be at the top. He'll be able to see the other side, that's what he wants."

"He can't, it's too big for him. Is he in trouble?" she asked again, and this time Andrew didn't answer.

"Stay here," she said. "Stay here and keep your eye on him. Do. Not. Move." She pulled her frizzy hair into a pony tail and fastened it with a rubber band from her pocket, tightened her sneaker laces, and started climbing, making her way quickly up the broad ledges at first, then losing the path, backtracking, sliding down to another level when a path thinned, ran out into sheer air. In places, there were recognizable steps gouged into the softer layers of baked mud and ash. Other times, she had to just claw her way up, digging her fingers into the harsh flesh of the formation. She used Andrew as a reference point to make sure that she wasn't going too far in either direction as she tacked back and forth, though it soon made her dizzy to look down at him, tiny on the immense prairie floor.

What had looked simple from the ground was actually a maze of crevices and narrow ledges. Yet tourists got up there every day. It wasn't a place for technical climbing, it didn't demand superb strength or skill to keep moving more-or-less upward. The canvas and rubber shoes she was wearing were quite sufficient. Even as she climbed higher, the not-quite-stone, not-quite-earth that crumbled under her shoes and fingernails was sometimes deliberately carved away from the true stone skeleton, forming manageable footholds and handholds. Even so high above the prairie that she would not have recognized Andrew if she hadn't known the speck of red was him, she told herself there was nothing remarkable about her situation. This wasn't Mount Everest.

But still she was horrified by the emptiness behind her as she clung to the rock wall. It felt as if she had ventured into a region utterly hostile to living things. She still couldn't see Colin, and only the fixed point of Andrew far below assured her that she was climbing in the right direction.

But what if Andrew wasn't fixed? What if he had been running along the base of the formation, following her, stopping when she stopped to look down? She shoved the thought out of the way and hauled herself upward. She tried calling out Colin's name every so often, but she didn't have the breath she needed, and anyway it felt as if a full shout vould blow her off into space, could maybe blow them both off into space. She didn't want to frighten him.

And then he was there, only twenty or thirty feet above her, though a broad, seemingly impassible crevice separated them. He hadn't noticed her yet. He had wedged himself into the space between the boulder and the spire that towered above it. He edged up a little way forward, then retreated a little way.

She waited until she couldn't stand it anymore and said his name. Then she said it a little louder, easing over to him with her voice as she could not see how to do with her body. Finally he looked around and spotted her. He waved cautiously, and Rita wanted to shriek at him for taking a hand off the mountain.

"Hey Mom," he called to her. He didn't seem scared, but he was obviously tired, the front of his shirt and shorts and his knees and sneakers brown with the grit of baked mud and crumbly stone. "I'm almost there," he said.

"Colin, you have to come down now," she said. "You've done a great climb, and now you have to come down."

He surprised her by not arguing, just turned and eased himself into the boulder's curve again and moved down a little. And then moved up again. She saw what was wrong. He couldn't find a foothold to get down from the narrow ledge at the boulder's base. He was too small to reach any support that his foot could catch, and at this height from the desert floor, the thought of dropping—even a few feet—was unbearable. He moved down a little, then up.

"Wait," she said. "How'd you get across there?" He twisted his head around to look at the steep slope beneath him, then pointed a finger uncertainly at a ridge of stone that angled up the wall of the big crevice separating them. "Honey, can you lower yourself to that?" He stared down at it, then looked away. It was so thin, it scarcely threw a shadow. He looked away from her.

She would have to get to him. It wasn't impossible. It was just sliding one foot, then the other, along that almost invisible line of shadow. Then doing it again. Then doing it again. Face pressed against the rough rock, trying to give gravity some help in sticking her to the mountain, Rita edged forward, all of space hauling at her back. She slid one foot forward, then the other, her outstretched hands creeping along the rock face. She kept on edging forward, and when she thought she was close enough, she fumbled blindly with her right hand as high as she could reach until she felt the rubber bumper of Colin's shoe. It was the sweetest thing she had ever touched. She squeezed it, felt his thin toes inside, and had to close her eyes for a moment.

"It's not too bad," she said. "Not bad at all." She was finally able to cautiously lift her face and look up at him. He was right there, right above her. "Now, I'm going to help you slide down to this ledge next to me," she said. "Turn around so your tummy is against the wall. I'll watch your feet." He maneuvered himself around until he was facing the wall. "Turn your hat around," she said. "I want you kissing that goddamn rock." He carefully turned the bill of his cap to the back, pressed himself against the boulder again. "Now slide your right foot back a little, and I'll guide it down. Then just let yourself slide down to the ledge next to me."

She felt the gritty, ribbed sole of his sneaker settle into her palm. She cupped it in her hand, lowered it until his other leg must have bent. She could feel him trembling with the strain, could see grit clinging to the almost invisible hairs of his hard, narrow calf. "Now ease your weight into my hand, and just slide down."

"You won't be able to hold me."

"I can hold you."

"You can't. You can't. We'll both fall."

"Colin," she said. She forced herself to breathe. "Pumped as I am at this moment, I could hold you and Andrew both. I could hold Walt."

Colin took a breath, eased his weight into the palm of Rita's hand, slid the other foot backward into space. Rita drove her shoulder into the crumbly not-quite-rock and kept her balance, not letting go of Colin's foot, bending with it, until the other foot thumped onto the ledge beside her, and even then he had to tug on it a little before she could let go, straighten up, and lead him by the hand along the thin shadow back to the other side of the crevice.

They worked their way down to where the ledge was wide enough for them to sit side by side and rest their backs against the rock wall. They were still breathtakingly high. "You know," Colin said, "I could have got down from there on my own. I got up and I could have got down."

"I know," she said. "You're a great climber."

"I almost made it. I almost got to see what's on the other side of this mountain."

"You don't think it's pretty much the same as what's on this side?" She gestured out toward the endless prairie that spread yellow-green into the distance, sweeping from the shadowed base of the formation to the far irregularities of the horizon. Hills or mountains, she didn't know what to call them. She had stopped trembling, but she wasn't ready yet to face the long climb down.

"I think it's different," Colin said. "This mountain is different, and I think what's on the other side is different. Hey, I can see Andrew! He's waving."

Rita looked down, couldn't find him in the shadows. She didn't need to. She knew he was down there. Colin was waving his arms above his head, crossing and uncrossing them in a slow semaphore. Rita looked at him, his long, soft brown face, hair sticking out stiffly, starched and tawny with dust, a clump of it thrusting forward through the adjustment hole in his backwards baseball cap. Bruce's delicate bones, his black, liquid eyes. The boys had almost none of her German solidness.

She stood up and pressed her palm against the ribbed top and center button of Colin's cap when he started to get up with her. "Wait here a minute, will you?" she said. "I want to check something out. Rest here a few more minutes."

"Okay, sure."

"Stay put. I mean it."

"I said, 'Sure.'"

She moved back up the thin path toward the boulder where Colin had been stuck. She pulled herself up to his ledge and worked her way up the groove where the boulder rested against a steeple of stone. She was just tall enough to reach a handhold, a crack that ran through the boulder. She pulled herself up, and edged forward on her belly till she could see over the boulder's top.

Rita closed her eyes after a while, then opened them again. She lay there and stared. She lay there on the warm rock and stared down at a vast, unbelievable expanse of gorges winding around sheer needles of rock, a stone forest spreading out as far as she could see, the prairie's soft flesh carved away, gouged down to the spiky skeleton of the earth, a hundred times more alien than the surface of the moon, more beautiful and terrifying than the landscape of paradise, calling her by name.

Rita Vogel stared and stared, until she heard the high, pure voice of her son sailing out into space, pleading for slow and gentle rocking, complaining about little Willie's refusal to go home, the sound thin and bare in the immense emptiness, the other half of his harmony inaudible to her, floating up from the desert floor.

FURIOUS

THERE WERE DAYS when Henry felt like the most cruelly betrayed, pissed upon man on the face of the earth. And then there were days when he felt blessed. Days like today. Today he was fastening bicycles like sails onto the roof of his wife's car, preparing for a ride with his children. A good father, a man who had been blessed.

It was a new feeling, still naked and unashamed. A few weeks before, walking out to the hospital parking lot after his chemo follow up, he had seen some orderlies crouched next to his car, looking underneath it and laughing. Rage had clenched its fist in his guts and he froze, torn between the urge to roar an obscenity at them and the colder, angrier impulse to slip up silently and catch them in the act, whatever the act was, get their asses fired. Before he could do either, the orderlies stood up and headed back to work, taking last drags on their cigarettes, joking, the whites among them as obnoxiously loud as the blacks.

Stepping forward, he had realized that it wasn't his car at all but one identical to his deep green Mercedes-Benz, which he had had to park beyond the spaces reserved for doctors. Some asshole from St. Mary's had parked in his usual spot, a Miata-driving jackal exploiting his diminished schedule.

He had reached his own car, unlocked the door, and stood there for a moment with his hand resting on the sun-warmed roof. Then he walked back to the other Mercedes. He squatted and peered into the shadows underneath it and found himself face to face with two raccoons hunched next to a dead squirrel, which they were evidently eating. Had been, anyway, until they were interrupted, first by the orderlies and then by him.

Getting over his first revulsion, he had stared at them, and they stared back. They must have come up from the steep, wooded banks of the Mississippi, which curved to within a block or so of his Minneapolis hospital. He didn't think they would have killed the squirrel, just came upon its corpse and tucked in. Or maybe they had found him crippled by injury or slowed down by old age or disease. A goner, one way or another. A meal.

As he crouched there in front of that horrid little tableau, something had surged through him, loosening every joint in his body. For a while he didn't dare stand up for fear of passing out, the emotion was so powerful, stronger than the grief he had felt at the deaths of his parents or the stillbirth of his now-almost-forgotten first child, not to mention other, lesser deaths—of relatives and colleagues, patients, public figures he admired. If he had been the sort of man who cried, it would have ripped tears out of him so hot they would have steamed down his cheeks as he squatted there on the freshly-lined asphalt. When he could straighten up and return to his car, he sat for what must have been a long time with his hands hooked over the steering wheel, trembling idiotically, before pulling himself together again and driving home.

He had, of course, known what it was. He didn't need the shrink to tell him it was his own approaching death by brain tumor he was grieving, his body the one being eaten beneath that car. But his pity had not been focused entirely on the squirrel. It included the raccoons, looking up from their dinner and peering at him from behind those masks, with innocence in their black, beady eyes. His innocence.

He had had a good day soon after this, then other good days. The brooding darkness he had been carrying around ever since his diagnosis two months earlier did not disappear, but its unyielding hold on him had been cracked, it came and went now like bad radio reception. As certain as ever that the surgery, radiation, and chemotherapy protocols he had endured had done no more than delay the glioblastoma that was killing him, he found himself visited by grace of an unexpected sort, not a reprieve from his death sentence, but pardon for the shortcomings of his life.

Over the years he had been accused of arrogance, of intolerance, of being a bully. He had had affairs, neglected his kids. What he now realized was that he had simply been acting according to his nature. He was a part of the fallen world, and like the rest of the world, he was entitled to forgiveness. With this liberating insight, a great peace had visited him. The years he had spent building his practice, doing his research, earning his reputation as a premier thoracic surgeon—they were over now. The time he had left was his redemption. Time to be a proper father, a good husband. A blessing, a man who was blessed.

"What shall we do?" That was the question, exotic in its simplicity, he could now offer to his children—Joseph, eight, and Samantha, thirteen. They didn't know, they weren't used to it yet. A movie, they suggested, which bored him, or going to the Mall of America, which was worse. They used to talk about wanting to go on bike rides, he reminded them, not just around the neighborhood, but on the paved trails that wound through the city parks. They liked that idea, and he had gone out and bought the best roof rack he could find and had it mounted on Penny's Saab, with carriers for four bikes, and bought himself and Penny new mountain bikes, lighter and more efficient than their old ones, which he had found he could barely wrestle onto the roof rack.

He had studied a book of bike trail maps and chosen for their first ride one that started in Hidden Falls Park—seven miles of asphalt trails snaking through the woods along the Mississippi. He followed the river's course with his finger, stuttering an invisible dotted line along the loop of water slung between St. Paul and Minneapolis. The river was more than an accident of geography, he understood now, more than a historical presence. It was as much a part of him as his blood vessels and nerves. He was continuous with it. On a good day, he was continuous with the universe.

Samantha asked if she could invite one of her friends. Henry much preferred for it to be just his family, but he said sure, they would pick her up on the way to Hidden Falls. Penny didn't want to go. She never felt comfortable riding a bike, she said. She didn't trust him not to tease her about how she rode, he thought. In the early years of their marriage, he had tried to get her to improve her form, her seat always adjusted too low to be efficient, feet splayed out like a duck's. Now she couldn't accept his newly-discovered harmony, though she wouldn't say so. "Are you sure you're up to it?" she had asked him, as if that was what concerned her, his physical stamina. It made him smile.

After breakfast, he backed the Saab out of the garage, hoisted his new bike onto the roof rack and clamped it down, went for Samantha's bike, then Joseph's. It was a job he could still handle. He could still drive a car, ride a bike. He went back inside. Penny was making them a picnic lunch. "Sure you don't want to join us? Perfect day." She shook her head, concentrating on the celery she was dicing for their tuna fish sandwiches. Her straight auburn hair swung forward like a curtain, shielding her face from him as she made the big chef's knife dance through the pale stalks.

It wasn't really a perfect day. The sky was overcast, and there was a hint of rain in the air, but that was just weather. If it rained, it rained, he said to his children as they piled into the car. With his left hand he reached to hit the garage door remote and found that Penny had taken it from the driver's side door pocket, where he had always kept it when this was his car, and had clipped it to the visor. He moved it back to the door pocket. Here his hand found it automatically, and he pushed the ribbed button. If it rained, they would just get wet, he said. So what?

Samantha said that she didn't want to get wet, and Joseph recalled when he had crashed his bicycle once after riding through puddles that had made his brakes slippery. They could stay home, he said to them, stopping the garage door before it reached the bottom. It was their choice. They said they wanted to go. He let the garage door finish closing.

They found Hannah's house in the Selby-Dale neighborhood

where he and Penny had lived before Joseph was born, and he loaded her bicycle into the fourth carrier. He liked how the bikes looked up there, poised upright together as if being raced through the air by ghosts. Samantha made Joseph switch places with her so that she could sit in the back with her friend.

Hannah was a small, delicately rounded girl who made the gangly, awkward Samantha look athletic by contrast. Like Samantha, she affected a bored, world-weary tone of voice when talking about school, friends, boys. The prematurely bitchy edge of their chatter grated on Henry's nerves, but it faded after they had worked through the topics of most aggressive social discrimination and turned to things more particular to them—good and bad babysitting jobs, piano lessons, painting their rooms. It always made him happy to see that his children had friends—happy, and somehow surprised.

They passed the sprawling Ford plant, then dropped down the steep road leading into Hidden Falls Park. Henry gestured toward a couple who were pushing bikes up the hill, their heads down like oxen. "Look at them sissies," he joked. "I'm twice their age and half dead, but at least I know what a mountain gear is for." Samantha stared out the window in silence and Hannah laughed politely.

But Joseph looked at him uneasily. "I read a sign back there says you're supposed to walk your bike on this hill," he said.

"That's for going down, so you don't kill yourself. I guarantee you, Joey, you wouldn't lose control riding up this hill. Maybe lose consciousness."

"Wait, I know this place," Samantha shouted, her face pressed against the window. "This is Down by the Bay!" Joseph looked around in confusion. "We came here sometimes when I was little," Samantha explained to Hannah. "There's like a bay, and we'd sing this Raffi song, 'Down by the Bay,' and we called this place Down by the Bay. Joey, don't you remember?"

Joseph stared around and nodded, imagining that he remembered. Henry did remember. After Joseph was born, Penny had had sort of a nervous breakdown, severe post-partum depression, and at the suggestion of her counselor they had gone on outings every weekend for a while. It stunned him that he hadn't made the connection earlier. Samantha was right, they had never called the park by its real name. It was always Down by the Bay.

At the bottom of the hill, they passed the enormous concrete picnic pavilions, in one of which dangled a pink and orange piñata. Henry could see coolers and grocery bags on the tables, but no people. Mexican or Central American immigrants, he guessed, off playing soccer or fishing in the river. He thought of the immigrants' children, blindfolded, wild with greed, swarming around the garish burro and clubbing it to pieces with a baseball bat.

Eight years. Penny had been the one in trouble then. He passed up the first parking lot, which was too far from the river, and drove to the lot designated for cars with boat trailers. As he lifted down the bikes, Samantha announced that she wanted to go check out the river. She also thought that they should eat right away so that the sandwiches wouldn't get soggy, but Henry pointed out that if it was going to rain, they would want to have finished their ride already. They could always eat their picnic in one of the pavilions. The river would always be there.

They set out on the smooth asphalt path, Joseph on his small bike pedaling madly to stay in front, then the two girls, who rode side by side, taking up the whole path. Henry kept to the rear, the buck letting his does and fawns precede him into a clearing so he can keep a protective eye on them.

However, Joseph soon got so far ahead that Henry lost sight of him as the trail wound through the woods. He drew up behind Samantha and Hannah and called out, "On your left!" Samantha looked around in confusion, swerved, and almost side-swiped Hannah, who wobbled off the trail for a moment. Samantha got her bike under control, jumped off, and screamed at him for nearly making her crash.

He stopped. "Settle down, Samantha. It's what you're supposed to say when you need to pass someone. You should be riding single file, anyway, on the right. What if someone came around a curve from the other direction?" They had met no one so far, probably because of the threatening weather, but it was a fair question. Samantha was trembling. "You okay?" he asked. "Hannah?" Hannah nodded. "Okay," he said, "I have to catch up with Joey, he needs to stay with us."

Henry took off again and pedaled hard, watching for sand that might have washed over the trail, knowing that Joseph would ignore it. The trail through the woods along the river was generally flat, but there were humps and dips and several tight curves, one of them swinging right out to the eroded lip of the river bank. When he finally caught sight of Joseph, waiting for them at the top of a long hill, he felt sharp, almost painful relief, and hoped that Samantha and Hannah weren't too far behind. "Wait!" he shouted to Joseph, seeing him lean forward to take off again.

The hill was difficult enough that Henry couldn't say anything more until he reached the top. He grabbed Joseph's handlebar and gave it a shake for emphasis. "You have to stay with us. You can't just go off on your own. What if it started raining? What if you crashed into the river? You could do that, you know, if you slipped on one of those turns. You want to drown?"

Joseph stared at him. "No," he said, "of course I don't want to drown."

"Well, then, stay with us."

"Did you see how I got like all the way up this hill?"

"If you hadn't like been so far ahead, I like would have seen you like do it."

"Well, I did it," Joseph said. "I used my gears."

"You like used your gears?"

"I used them."

"Good," Henry said, softening. "Good for you, Joey. Now, how long do you think it will take those poor girls to catch up with us?"

It took them quite a while—they must have deliberately dawdled. Finally they came into sight and struggled up the hill. Then the four of them went on together. The trail passed a construction site with earth-moving equipment. It ran along the base of a sheer sandstone cliff that had two huge doors set into it like a giant's cave in a fairy tale, then plunged back into what seemed like deeper woods along the floor of the river valley. It was starting to sprinkle a little, but Henry wanted to reach a lake that he had seen on the map, probably once a backwater of the river, though now cut off from it.

The threatening weather kept them together. Joseph now made a point of stopping and letting the others catch up whenever he found himself well ahead or whenever the trail forked, and the girls mostly rode single file. When they reached the lake, it was swampy with cattails and blanketed with bright green algae from shore to shore. It wasn't much of a destination, but Henry was tired and made the kids get off their bikes and hike around a little, exploring while he rested on the warm asphalt. The occasional sprinkles were coming more regularly, becoming a light drizzle. The day was warm enough that it felt soft, like a caress, and none of the children complained. After a little while they all got on their bikes again and headed back.

Henry wondered how things would go if a real downpour developed, but by the time they made it back to the picnic grounds, it had stopped again. He was exhausted, and considered leaving the bike-loading until after they had eaten. If it started to pour, however, the job would be even worse, so he wrestled the bikes back up onto the roof rack while the children took the picnic things out and ran to claim a table. He made them change to one closer to the boat-loading ramp, then let Samantha take charge of setting the table and distributing the food and soft drinks. They had no tablecloth, but the aluminum picnic table looked new and reasonably clean. He couldn't remember what sort of tables there had been eight years before. Filthy, scarred old wooden ones, probably. Something sticky and distasteful clung to his memory of those picnics.

He was so tired now, he had little appetite, just sipped at a can of mineral water while the kids ate chips and fooled around with the sandwiches and leaped up screaming every time a yellowjacket swooped in and landed on a can of soft drink or glob of tuna. When they were done, Samantha asked if she could be excused, and the three children headed down to the river to skip stones. Henry forced himself to eat half of a sandwich, cleaned up the mess of crumbs and wrappers, and sat down again.

The river bank was too steep for him to see the children from where he was sitting, but he could hear them shouting and laughing, and the clack of rocks. He sat there, looking at his wonderful hands spread before him on the ribbed aluminum of the picnic table. He watched the little tremor in his wrists. Finally he got up and walked over to the bank and found a place to scramble down to the shore.

None of the kids was any good at skipping stones. The girls threw like, well, like girls, and Joseph chose stones that were too large to do anything but arc a few feet and make a big splash. Henry pulled the boy aside and showed him the sort of stone to look for, flat discs of shale about the size of a silver dollar, and demonstrated how to grip it with thumb and forefinger wrapped around the thin edge, and how to fling it sidearm, with a snap of the wrist, the rock sailing out and touching the water and leaping up again and touching and leaping, leaving a graceful curve of ripple points disappearing into the surface, each leap quicker and shorter than the last.

"Five!" Joseph screamed. "Dad got five skips!" It was more like seven or eight, but Henry didn't bother to correct him, just threw a few more, even better ones, while Samantha and Hannah were watching. Samantha was impressed and got him to show her the right kind of stone to look for, and in a few minutes all of them were doing better, though then for some reason Samantha started to throw the stones backhanded, like a Frisbee, and no matter how Henry explained that she couldn't get any power that way, she persisted, managing to get a few skips and shrieking with pride.

Irritated, Henry gave up and climbed back up the sandy, eroded bank and found a place to sit on a protruding cottonwood root, where he could watch them. A motor boat skimmed by, sending trails of wake to comb against the shoreline. From farther up the river, some other kids appeared, about a dozen of them, working their way down the rocky beach. They were dark, Asian or Hispanic he thought at first, then saw that they were black, boys and a few girls, about Samantha's age, probably. Some of the boys were shirtless, their chests thin and polished looking, their heads either shaved or wild with dreadlocks.

He tensed and waited for Samantha to notice the new kids and retreat from the river back up to the safety of grass and picnic table and adult protection. She and Hannah kept on searching for good, flat stones, however, flinging them out into the river, laughing and leaping around when one skipped a few times. Joseph moved to the other side of his sister and her friend, away from the approaching kids. He was more obviously eyeing them, but kept on tossing stones.

The bank where Henry was sitting was maybe twenty feet above the silty, rocky beach. He knew he should go down and stop trouble before it started, but he waited a few minutes more while the new kids came closer. He had grown up in a mixed neighborhood in Chicago and had had his share of fights in the park a few blocks from his house. Mostly he had fought other white kids, but he had always been more afraid of the blacks who shared the park. They were his classmates, many of them, and they got along all right at school, yet he always had the feeling that they would hurt him if they could. He didn't know why, and he had survived his childhood without it happening, but the cold swirl of danger in his guts now was as familiar as the sound of his parents' voices calling him in to supper or ordering him to bed.

Still, he waited. Neither group acknowledged the other. Some of the black kids began tossing rocks into the river, too. They slowed as they approached Samantha and Hannah and Joseph. By the time the closest was only about ten feet away, the group had stopped. They roughhoused with each other, and more of them started picking up rocks and throwing them into the river, not skipping them, just rearing back and hurling them as far out as possible. Several were wearing backward or half-backward baseball hats, a gang thing or fashion, Henry didn't know which.

Joseph sometimes went around that way, too, though he was bareheaded now, since he had had to wear a helmet while biking. Henry had told him wearing a hat backward could get him beat up if the wrong people saw it, but really the problem was that it looked stupid. It made anyone look stupid, even his own son. Watching the boy from above, he suddenly remembered walking with him along this same beach, carrying him in a corduroy baby carrier strapped to his chest, waiting for Penny to snap out of it. He remembered looking down and seeing the top of the sleeping baby's head, misshapen, bald except for an almost invisible down. He wasn't sure Penny ever had snapped out of it, not completely, though she had gotten over the worst of it.

Most of the kids were throwing stones into the water by now. One of the black girls was close enough to Samantha that when they hunted around they were working the same section of beach. That was where it could start, Henry thought, competing over a damn rock, and he edged toward a gully that cut through the lip of the bank, where he had gotten down to the beach before. He wasn't sure how much he could do if there was real trouble, but he had a vision of himself charging down on them like an avenging angel.

Samantha picked up a rock, walked to the very edge of the river, wound up for one of her awkward backhand throws, and sent the rock sailing out over the water. One, two, threefourfive skips, a miracle. She whooped and did a little dance of triumph, and Hannah clapped. Without glancing at her, the nearest black girl picked up a flat rock big as a saucer. She walked forward, stopping a few feet from where Samantha was standing. She coiled her body, and flung the big stone with that same backhand Frisbee motion, and they all watched it sail out and hit the water and lift and skip three or four more times. Hannah and Samantha clapped, and the girl shouted something to her friends.

A speedboat roared into sight, heading up river. Some of the kids waved and some threw rocks that might have been aimed at the boat. The rocks fell far short, but the intensity of the throwing seemed to increase. By the time the boat had disappeared around a bend of the river, all of the children were throwing rocks, some still trying to skip them at first, but then just flinging them out into the river, no more searching around for the perfect stone, now, throwing anything— handfuls of pebbles, rocks the size of grapefruit, pieces of driftwood, beer cans half full of silt, anything they could get their hands on they hurled into the river. There was something horrible about it. It was as if they hated the river, as if they were trying to kill it, and Henry could barely tell his own children from Hannah or the black kids, they were that united in their frenzy, hurling stone after stone at the river, furious.

They threw and threw, not even screaming and laughing any- more, as if they couldn't spare breath from the job of filling the river with stones. If it hadn't started raining, it seemed that they would have thrown until their hands bled from clawing rocks out of the hard-packed silt or they fainted with exhaustion. As it was, they didn't break and run until the rain turned to a downpour. The black kids headed upriver again, and Joseph and Samantha and Hannah scrambled back up the bank and ran for the car. Henry followed them in a kind of daze, and had a hard time getting the doors un- locked, the children crowded around him in such agitation.

Settling himself behind the wheel, Henry congratulated himself on having gotten all the bikes fastened onto the roof rack before it started raining, though it was unpleasant to think of them standing up there, exposed to the storm. It didn't bother the kids. Once they had themselves strapped in, their excitement boiled up again, and they were all laughing and shouting while the rain pounded against the windows. "God," Samantha exclaimed, "I never had so much fun." The other two agreed—none of them had ever had such a good time.

"You didn't mind getting wet?" Henry asked, watching the top of the girls' heads bob in the rearview mirror.

"*Hell* no!" Samantha shouted, and Hannah and Joseph laughed. Carried along on the high of her own boldness, Samantha launched into the Raffi song—"Down by the bay, where the watermelons grow, back to my home, I dare not go, for if I do, my mother will say—" And paused for the good part, where somebody had to supply the mother's insane, rhyming question. Samantha finished it with one from the record—"'Did you ever see a fly, wearing a tie?'" and they all joined in on the concluding "Down by the bay!" They sang verse after verse all the way to Hannah's house, recalling other favorite lines. "'Did you ever see a whale with a polka dotted tail?'" "'Did you ever see a llama eating its pajamas?' Down by the bay!"

After Henry had unloaded Hannah's bike in the driving rain and seen her disappear with it into the garage behind the old frame four-square, he got back in and found Joseph and Samantha still singing the song, now improvising punch lines, mostly lame ones. "Did you ever see a tree, big as a bee?" But some were pretty good. "Did you ever see a river that tasted like liver?'" "'Did you ever see a table big as Aunt Mabel?'" Henry joined in on the choruses, and once in a while supplied the question. "'Did you ever see a Penny who didn't have any?'" he sang when the kids paused to give him a turn. "'Did you ever see a surgeon who could swim like a sturgeon?' Down by the bay!"

He was working on another one when he turned onto their own block, the rhythm of the windshield wipers and the giddy singing of his children wrapping him in a cloak of happiness. They would remember this day forever, he thought, a perfect day after all. When his kids had their own kids, they would take them for a bike ride sometime and remember him, a good father, who gave them the best day of their lives.

"Down by the bay," he sang along with them, "where the watermelons grow." Without having to look, he reached down with his left hand into the door pocket and pressed the garage door remote control at exactly the right moment before swinging the car into the driveway, his old timing still perfect, and accelerated toward the rising door that would reach the top just as he sailed under it into the shelter of the garage. "Back to my home," they sang, and another kind of music crashed down like an avalanche and enveloped them, an orchestra of sound as dense in the moment as a thunderclap, the bright shriek of splintering doorframe and the blare of tortured metal tubing, percussion of spokes snapping and tires exploding, the music of the end of the world.

WHAT IT WAS

THE NOISE HAD been loud enough to yank them out of the first shallows of sleep. To Walt, it sounded like a balloon popping. Rita thought that somebody had smashed one of her windows again. She thought they would find a rock or chunk of asphalt on the floor downstairs in a litter of broken glass, a breeze pushing in through the jagged hole. It would be the third time.

He said, "It sounded like a balloon." Her twins, Andrew and Colin, had celebrated their eleventh birthday the week before, and there might have been balloons left over. He lay in the darkness, knowing that balloons don't just pop in the middle of the night. In the middle of the night they lie in the darkness, maybe stirring vaguely in a draft like sleepers, exhaling imperceptibly, going dull, shrinking into limp membranes damp on the inside with somebody's week-old breath. He didn't think this, but he knew it. They don't just pop.

She was waiting for him to check it out. "Put something on your feet," she said after he sat up finally and swung his legs over the side of the bed. When his toe touched the discarded condom, he nudged it aside, then reached down and tossed it into the wastebasket. He was naked, still a little sweaty from their lovemaking. He found the bathrobe draped over the end of the bed, thrust his feet into his work boots, and shuffled out into the hallway, careful not to step on the trailing leather laces.

He stood outside the twins' closed door, listening, then went to the bathroom and urinated. He tied the boot laces around his bare ankles so he wouldn't trip, and went downstairs, noting the little blink of red light when he passed the new security system's movement sensor, armed, but in the "stay" mode, tolerating movement inside the house.

Her study window had been the first. She and her boys had been in the house only about a month. He was having supper with them at the kitchen table when they heard a sudden bright noise from the front of the house. She was getting something from the refrigerator and went to see what the noise was. "What was it?" Colin asked when she came back, and Andrew said, "Yeah, it sounded like music." She waved her hand in casual disgust and said that a window had gotten broken, then put away the milk and sat down and ate.

Afterward, she was trembling with anger when she showed Walt the screen and storm window that had been smashed, the unbroken wine cooler bottle lying in the window casing where it had fallen, stopped by the main sash, the aluminum screen with a perfect silhouette of the bottle torn through it sideways, like in a cartoon.

The second time was a few months later, after they had started sleeping together. It woke them in the middle of the night, and they came downstairs together to find a flagstone from the side garden lying under the dining room table, glass all over the room. It was a big stone, ten or fifteen pounds, one of a pickup load Walt had hauled in and laid for her in paths winding through her new gardens. While she swept up glass, he went down to the basement and cut a piece of plywood to temporarily fill the window opening. The next day he had removed from the exposed side garden all the flagstones except those even somebody as big as he was would have had trouble throwing. He had laid the smaller stones inside the fence and replaced them with back-breakers that rode deep in the garden soil, like icebergs.

He wondered now why she hadn't gotten up with him to investigate this time. Maybe she thought she carried a kind of jinx, being the one who found trouble, or maybe she was less worried this time, or more worried. He had a theory that the vandals had been challenged by the old security company stickers that a previous owner had affixed to several vulnerable windows. The bottle through her study window had missed one of those stickers by only inches, and the flagstone had probably been too heavy to reach its target on the upper sash. He still had the bottle and the improbably torn screen in his workshop, and the flagstone was now holding up one of her potted plants in the dining room. It seemed important to him to keep these things close by, even now that there was an actual security system in place.

Without turning on the light, he went into her study and snapped up the shade. Nothing was wrong here, and nothing was wrong in the living room or the dining room or the kitchen or the pantry, which he checked in turn, each time peering out of the darkened room into the emptiness of the lamp-lit sidewalk and street or the heavily fenced back yard.

He made the rounds a second time, moving from window to window like a great, silent bear, trying to catch sight of something, somebody in a parked car out on the dark street, a drunk, a kid, any-body suspicious. Though relatives and old friends had cautioned Rita against buying a house so deep in the inner city, it was generally a good neighborhood—racially mixed, with mostly owner-occupied housing—and the incidents of vandalism had shocked her. Walt told her it wasn't personal: people everywhere just did stupid things.

Rita had bought the house after her husband died and she moved back to the U.S. She had hired Walt out of the Yellow Pages, more or less at random, to do the renovation. Six months later, he had moved in with her, the first stable relationship he had had since his second wife divorced him, ten years before. He had stopped drinking after that divorce, but had not allowed himself to fall in love again until he met Rita.

The noise wasn't a broken window. He had never thought it was—the sound was wrong, a pop, not a shattering. He would have to check the upstairs windows, but with a tall old house like this, it would be hard to break one of those with a rock.

Before going upstairs, he stepped out onto the front porch and lit a cigarette. It was a soft May night. He tightened the cord of the bathrobe and walked out to the street corner, listening to the soothing hum of traffic from the freeway a few blocks north, the almost inaudible rise and fall of a siren that might have been miles away.

There were no lights on in any of the neighbors' houses. The old street lamps glowed at their proper intervals down the block, down the next block, the one beyond that, then out of sight, dropping below the curvature of the night. At the corner, instead of going back, he turned and followed the sidewalk toward the rear of the house. Passing the side garden, he looked up at the red shield of the old security company, still affixed to the dining room window's upper sash. The hosta and ferns and daylilies were sprouting in this garden by now, but their green leaves were as invisible in the night as their roots spreading among the massive blocks of yellow Mankato stone.

He reached the end of the backyard fence and the garage he had built for Rita. The doors were closed, and there were no windows. Inside, he knew, his truck and Rita's car stood side by side in the darkness, undisturbed. He decided to continue around the block, telling himself he was still investigating the sound that had woken them, but really just enjoying the mild spring night. And if someone looked out and saw him walking by in his bathrobe and work boots? They would have to accept him for what he was, a man awake in the middle of the night, going for a walk. A big white man in a bathrobe, having a smoke. It was no crime to go for a walk at night. Maybe being outside without pants was, but he had no intention of opening the robe.

Turning at the far end of the block, he saw movement ahead, an animal crossing the street, breaking into a loping run when it noticed him. It looked like a cat, though it might have been a raccoon. The previous summer he had seen one disappear into the sewer opening in front of the house.

None of the neighborhood dogs was out. None barked at him, anyway. He studied each house as he passed it, considering it from a security point of view, noticing the ones with alarm system signs in their front yard, Brinks, ADT, Floyd, the houses with overgrown bushes where a burglar or rapist could hide, one with glass block basement windows of the sort he had been intending to put in as soon as he had the time, houses, like Rita's, with their original beveled glass front doors, and those with steel or solid wood replacements. The best security, he thought, was neighbors looking out for each other, which is what he was doing right now.

He met no one and noticed nothing unusual on his walk until, returning from the other direction, he saw the downstairs of Rita's house blazing with light and a police car parked in front, the blindingly bright strobe of its roof array pulsing. He broke into a run, awkward in the loosely tied boots, and pounded up the porch steps. A female cop met him at the door and with grim politeness asked him to identify himself. He could see another policeman in the kitchen, a black man, writing something in a log book, and Rita, looking terrible, clutching the phone to her mouth.

Fear exploded inside him like a heart attack. He heard himself shout something. He pushed past the first cop, lunged into the house, felt himself grabbed by the elbow and spun around, slammed into the entry wall so hard that a picture was knocked off and smashed to the floor. "Rita!"

She looked up, seeing him for the first time, as the cop did something excruciatingly painful to his arm and pushed him face first into the wall. She was half his size, but using some sort of vicious cop hold. Rita screamed at her to let him go, he was her husband, and then told him to close his robe.

"What's wrong?" he shouted, struggling to tie the robe's soft belt, having trouble with the arm the cop had almost twisted off. "Are you okay? Are the boys—"

She shook her head at him, furious or scared, he couldn't tell which. "You went out and triggered the alarm. I couldn't reach it before it went off, and then I thought I managed to get it turned off, but I guess I got the numbers wrong and hit the duress code. Jesus Christ, what were you doing? I was just talking to the alarm company. Where'd you go?"

He explained where he had gone, and told the cops about the noise, and the windows that had been broken in the past. They were so polite, so careful, it was clear they believed he had done some-thing wrong, something other than triggering the alarm system. The woman cop had Rita take her upstairs to check on the boys while the other stayed in the kitchen and kept asking him about how things were going, how they had been getting along, had he had a drink or two, were the two of them under particular stress lately. Questions like corpses, risen from the grave.

"I'm in A.A.," he told the cop. "I've been sober for nine years." The women were taking a long time. He knew what they were talking about. They were talking about him, the cop trying to coax an account of brutality out of Rita, checking for bruises, looking for signs of a struggle. Okay, that was her job. He knew what it looked like, how stupid it sounded, how bad it could be.

He went to the broom closet and saw the cop tense. "I'm going to clean up the glass." He got a broom and dustpan and carried a wastebasket to where the picture had fallen, one of Rita's old family photos, her grandparents hugging each other on their honeymoon. When he was almost done, the cop came and held the dustpan for him as he swept up the last shards. Then he went over the whole area with a damp paper towel the way his mother had taught him, who had cleaned up a lot of glass in her day. He fingered his shoulder joint.

"She had to react," the cop said. "Anything could have been going on. You're a big guy."

"Sure. I understand."

The boys slept through the whole thing. In the morning he told them about it, and they hooted in disappointment at missing the excitement. "That lady cop pinned you?" Andrew shouted. "Pinned *you*? Holy crap."

Colin thought of something. He left the table, rushed upstairs, and returned in a few moments with the remains of a purple balloon in his hand. "I had it tied to the back of my chair. It must've popped."

"Well, that's what it sounded like," Walt said.

"Sometimes," Andrew said, "what it sounds like is what it is."

A MAN IN TROUBLE

"It wasn't wrong to stop," I tell her. She has fallen asleep, drugged by the anger in her blood, leaving me to crawl around all night on the smoldering trash of our quarrel.

I say, "That part wasn't wrong."

"Didn't say wrong. Worse than wrong."

"Man flags you down, a man in trouble, you don't just check your door locks and floor it."

"A white man you've never seen before."

"What's that got to do with it?" A white man, I mean.

"You haven't learned a goddamn thing, have you? That man in Florida they poured gas on and burned mostly to death?"

"This wasn't—"

"A little boy sitting in his car seat right behind you? My little boy, my first baby, buckled into his car seat for safety? For *safety!*"

That's where it bursts into flames, I can never get past that, hard as I try. I try. "Sara," I say, "I wanted to show him we could afford to be generous, stop and listen to anyone's story. Show him what it means to belong somewhere."

"Well, you showed him."

•

I showed him. A cold, overcast afternoon, the day after Thanksgiving. As we slowed for the intersection a block away from home, a man appeared suddenly, waving his arms, cutting across the frozen boulevard to intercept us. A tall thin white man, forty-five, maybe fifty, in a torn nylon baseball jacket too light for the weather. A face that looked like it was made in a hurry. He forced a smile through the tangle of dirty creases as he leaned down and said something through the passenger side window. Ike, my six-year-old, made an impatient noise from the back seat.

•

THE DAY BEFORE, my parents, uncles, aunts, cousins, and cousins' children, and Sara's grandmother and brother and aunt had all joined us for Thanksgiving dinner. They had driven in from Bloomington and Richfield and Burnsville and Eagan—suburbs south of Minneapolis and St. Paul—and crowded into this tall old house in the inner city which Sara and I had spent the past fourteen months of our lives fixing and painting.

In the big kitchen where we set the kids' places and around the mightily-extended dining room table and later in the park across the street and in the living room watching the game, there had been a lot of joking about "the 'hood." They kept calling me "home boy," as if the term were hilarious applied to me, applied to any of us.

My cousins especially were entertained by the eccentricity of our migration back into the once-decaying neighborhood my wife's family had fled twenty years ago, the same one which my own father and his brothers, up from Missouri twenty-five years before that, had had the good sense to avoid from the start in favor of the raw, pioneer suburbs. There, if they weren't welcome, they were left alone, given plenty of space to fade into the blank-lawned developments.

My father wasn't entertained. He was permanently offended by my disregard for his advice and example. He thought my judgment had been bad enough when we bought a house in Merriam Park, a decent residential neighborhood of St. Paul that was about as white and middle class as his own suburb, but fifty years older, with more urban salt to it, houses two-storied, front-porched, alleyed. Drug stores and groceries within walking distance. When we moved east from there, straight into old Selby-Dale, he was almost struck dumb. He still identified it as the ghetto he had so brilliantly avoided. The house is only blocks away from buildings he had watched burn on television when I was in high school. Sara grew up in the neighborhood, and her family had moved away in 1976, when things were getting really rough. Afterward, it turned around again, but not in my father's eyes.

He was there when we first spotted the house, at Rondo Days, celebrating the mostly black community that had been ripped in half by I-94 in the sixties. Sara and I had been coming to the festival ever since we moved to St. Paul, but it was a surprise that my father and mother were there. They had parked at our house in Merriam Park, and we drove them over. It was a church thing, I think, a sister congregation had a tent, selling baked goods or doing missionary work. I remember my father complaining about the music pounding through the park, then working on a plate of ribs and catching up with a man he knew from back in St. Louis who had somehow recognized him. The man's son mentioned that there was a good house across the street about to go on the market. We went and took a look, stepping over the tangles of electric cables running down the street to amplifiers and concession trucks. The next day, I called the owner.

·

I LEANED OVER and lowered the window. An icy wind kicked in. I caught the man's smell, not awful, but brightly metallic, as if it originated in the tarnished silver fabric of his jacket rather than coming from his body. Over his heart there was a company or team name I couldn't make out, and a little below that a fist-sized hole had been burned and melted through the nylon shell, exposing scorched filler. His fingers hooked over the door were cracked and painful looking, the color of old radishes, and the frayed elastic of his cuffs curled back from his pale, thin wrists.

He stooped into the window. "Hey, my man," he said, not as jaunty as that sounds, even from a white guy. Tense, like his vocal cords had been broken once or twice. "Seemed there wasn't nobody in the world would stop for me," he said. "I'm about froze."

Looking past his seamed, wind-reddened face, I could see our icy park and in the distance swings swaying crazily from the playground equipment, and empty paths and empty sidewalks and not a single car, not a single moving thing except the swings and the desolate

leaves of some little crabapple trees the city had planted in a corner
of the park that summer.

I was taking Ike for an overnight with one of his classmates, glad
to get him out of the house, where he had been bored and whining.
I had expected that there would be kids playing in the park on this
school holiday, kids who would keep him occupied, but maybe it was
too cold, too dark all day, the bloated sky wanting to snow but too
half-hearted to get it going. It did seem like we were the only living
things for miles.

"What's the matter?"

"Accident," he said. "I hate asking for help, but I don't know what
else to do. Bless you for stopping." The car shook a little in a gust of
wind. The man hunched lower, drew himself deeper into the inad-
equate jacket. "We blown out a tire on the freeway. My wife's hurt,
they got her in the emergency room. I need to get back to Hudson.
Over in Wisconsin? Wife got the diabetes, and they took her to the
hospital. She's waiting for me. The cops said they can't take me home
since it's in Wisconsin. They can't go there. Regular, they take you
home if you have trouble. All my money's at home. I got to get home
so I can come back and pick up my wife and take care of her."

I said, "I can't drive you to Hudson. I have to get this boy somewhere. We're headed the opposite direction."

He nodded, sniffed, looked at Ike, then back at me again. His
eyes were watery, and what I guess you call hazel—brownish, with
fugitive glints of green and yellow. It's a sad color that made me
think of a Weimeraner our neighbors owned when I was a kid.

Another blast of wind struck the car, and Ike whispered, "Dad!
I'm getting cold!"

"I know, honey, hang on. Look," I said to the man, "we're going in
the opposite direction. Sorry." My neck was starting to cramp from
the way I was leaning over to talk with him. It made me uncomfortable, too, to see him stooped so far, a tall man. I wanted to get going,
but he had a hold on my car.

He stood there looking at me, seeming to struggle with something. "Well, listen, could you at least loan me something? So I could buy a used tire to get me back home?" I must have tightened up, because he rushed along, "I can get it back to you already this afternoon. You'll have your money in an hour. I just got to get back to Hudson where my own money is. I got enough, I'm working." The wind hit us again, billowing his jacket and riffling the pages of a library book I had on the dashboard. After dropping Ike off for his overnight, I was planning to go to a coffee shop and read for an hour or so.

"Dad! I'm freething!" Ike had a loose tooth that he was working on.

"Get in," I said to the man, "so we can close the window. Get out of the wind for a minute."

He scrambled in and cranked up the window. "Man," he said, "it is bitter! I like to die out there." He told me that he was a trucker, he had just begun working for 3M. He would leave his pager with me for security, he said. He took the pager out of his jacket pocket and handed it to me. I took it reluctantly, looked at it. There was no 3M logo or anything like that. But would there be? He took out a badly-worn leather wallet, showed me his driver's license, the photo recognizably him, even behind the yellowing plastic window. "If I'm leaving you my pager, you know I have to get that back, it's part of my job. You know what it's like to need a job."

I sat there, half-listening, and tried to think my way through a sludge of feelings that had risen up around me. He was probably trying to scam me, I had understood that right away, must have felt it even before I rolled down the window. Except how do you ever know? Really know.

•

IT WAS A familiar feeling. The first week we were in our house, an old woman I had seen around the neighborhood came by, asking for work. She needed to make five or ten dollars to buy food for herself and her granddaughter, she said. She would do anything, they were hungry. Didn't we have boxes to unpack? Floors to scrub? We did, of course, have boxes to unpack, more than I could stand to think about, and we hadn't even begun to address the question of the floors. But not wanting a stranger in the house when we were in such chaos, I loaned her ten dollars and she promised to repay me as soon as she got paid by a lady she had cleaned for that week. "I'm Maryanne!" she said. "Everybody know me around here, son. I live right around the corner, down Dayton, by the church."

Saturday, she came by with a personal check for twenty-five dollars to show me. "I'm taking this to the Unbank," she announced. "I'll buy some groceries and pay you back, both!" An hour later she returned with the check, her face distorted by confusion and anger. "They charging nine dollars just to cash it at the Unbank!" she cried. "What that leave me and my granddaughter, once I pay you off? Hardly squat." Her voice dropped, became something small and pathetic. "I wonder, do you have a bank, sir?" (Sir. She was as old as my grandma.) "Could you possibly cash this check for me?" Before I could answer, she dug into a bulging vinyl purse and pulled out a state identification card, which she thrust at me, proving she was herself. I felt blood suddenly roaring in my ears, rage against the Unbank and the crazy bind she was in because she was too poor to have a bank account. I had her endorse the check over to me and gave her fifteen dollars.

A week later, while we were having supper, Maryanne came by, ecstatic, and showed me a check for eighty-five dollars her ex-husband had sent her from Illinois. "I can pay you back," she said, "and I'm going to buy us some meat. I'm headed down to the Unbank this minute and then I'm going to pay you back in full and then I'm going to buy me some meat." I reminded her that she had already paid me back in full. She looked at me as if I were pulling her leg, but finally accepted it and put her scrawny, loose-skinned arms around me in a quick embrace, then practically ran down our porch stairs and off to the Unbank.

At ten o'clock, just as the news came on, the doorbell rang. It was Maryanne again, clutching the check and a file folder. She made me look through it—certificates from community education classes in

typing and accounting and household management and some letters
from Welfare and other papers I couldn't at a glance identify. She
was agitated, almost in tears. "Unbank won't cash this damn check,"
she yelled. "Out of town, they say. It got to be local, or they won't do
nothing." Her voice sank sickeningly again. "I wonder, sir, could you
find it in your heart to take this check and write me out a local one
they'll cash for me? I'll bless you all my life. I got to have this money.
It's about the first good thing that son of a bitch ever did for us, he
used to beat me, I had no choice, I had to leave him. I stuck with him
nineteen years!"

She had told me this about him before. Sara came down to see
what was going on, and Maryanne repeated the story to her until I finally stopped her and said, yes, I would write her a local check. "Bless
you, sir!" she said. "I'll pray to Jesus for you every day of my life! Both
of you! Jesus bless both of you!" Twenty minutes later, the phone rang.
It was the Unbank, calling to see if I had really written a check for
eighty-five dollars to a Maryanne George. Yes, I said, of course I had,
wasn't my name on it? I was barely able to choke down the anger I felt
surging back up my throat like bile.

"That's the last of Maryanne, I think," Sara said when I had hung
up.

"Maybe," I admitted, looking at the pale blue check from Solomon
George, Batavia, Illinois, with the memo, "for Gchilds Needs (Raye)."

"Why shouldn't it be good, though?" I asked.

Sara shrugged, "It's okay, baby. You're a decent man. Just so long as
you know how it is."

"She looks so much like my Grandma Magee."

"I know, baby. Come to bed."

It had been the last we saw of her, though the check returned in
a few weeks, stamped "Account Closed." I felt bad for Maryanne, as
if the man had struck her one more time. Later, there was the man
who came by and offered to paint our garage and never returned from
Sears, where I had sent him with twenty dollars for primer, and the
boy from down the block who borrowed a fishing rod I never saw

again and who once scammed Ike out of five dollars birthday money, and the stream of kids selling overpriced candy and bad light bulbs. "You're like that brother from another planet," Sara said to me. "I bet they can't believe you're really one of us."

"I'll send those Walkathon kids to you," I said. "You can carve up their lying butts for them."

"That's it," she said. "I'm from this neighborhood before it got nice again." She didn't really mind, though. She didn't mind that. But this white man. Why should that have mattered? We're hard enough on each other.

•

I SAID TO HIM, "Look, you don't know this area. Why don't I drive you to a filling station. There's one at Selby and Fisk. You can get out of the cold. Call somebody."

He shook his head. "I got nobody to call," he said. "The wife is all I got, and she's lying there in that emergency room wondering what's taking me so long. What I need is just thirty dollars to buy me a used tire that'll get me home." He looked at me with that face that seemed to have ropes twisted underneath the skin, then stared out the window. "I know what you're thinking," he said. "You're thinking, 'Who is this honky? Why should I help out this white motherfuck-er?'"

"Hey." I gestured angrily back at Ike, who was sitting there so quietly with his finger in his mouth, wiggling that tooth, the man might have forgotten about him.

He twisted around in his seat. "Sorry, fella, pardon my French." Ike just looked at him, and the man turned back to me. "Oh, man, I'm so upset, I don't know what I'm doing. I just really need that thir-ty dollars long enough to buy a tire and get home and get my money and come back. It'd take two hours, tops. You'd have my pager, man! You'd have my livelihood in your hand. You know what a job means to a man."

"I don't even think I have that much," I said. "Thirty dollars, I don't carry a lot of money around with me. I was just running my boy over to his friend's house."

"Couldn't you go to a cash machine?" he asked. "Couldn't you do that?"

I laughed, "No, I can't do that." I could feel Ike's impatience boiling against the back of my neck. When I turned to give him a reassuring smile, he mouthed something to me that I couldn't make out, probably, "Let's go!"

"We will," I said to him. "Don't worry. We'll be going in a minute."

The man was trying to scam me, I understood that. But I felt the need for the truth. If he was lying, I had to know it, I don't know why, nail him to it. And if not, I had to help him, a man in trouble.

"Listen," I said, watching his reaction, "maybe I should take you back to the hospital, see how your wife is doing."

"Dad." A tight whisper I chose to ignore.

"That's where I just come from," the man said. "I walked all this way from there in this bad weather. I ain't going back until I get what I got to get. She'd think I was crazy."

"Your car's where, again?"

"Side of the freeway."

"Close to the Dale exit? Farther downtown?"

"It's where I left it," he said. "It ain't going nowhere, shape it's in."

I could have driven along the freeway and seen if it was there, but what then? "How about if I just drive you to the 66 on Selby, we can see how much they'd charge you for a used tire."

"No," he said, "that would be too much. I know a guy who'll sell me one for thirty dollars, just got to get the money together." He scoured his fingers into his shadowed eye sockets as if trying to root out migraine. He said, "I'm not asking for charity, man, just a little faith, a little human trust. You won't be out a penny, I swear. Loan me what I need and I swear to God you'll have it back before suppertime." He was getting sweaty and miserable, and I was torn between feeling that I had him, I had just about nailed him, and that I was no better than the Unbank bastards who humiliated Maryanne George. He said, "You've seen trouble yourself sometime, I bet. You know what it feels like, everybody thinks they can yank you around, right, man? Am I right?"

I shrugged.

"Dad!"

"Hang on, Ike. I'm trying to think, how can we help here." I turned to the man, wanting to gauge his expression. "I don't have much on me, over what I need for food, but say if I loan you that and give you a lift to the guy who's going to sell you the tire?"

He was silent for a minute, staring ahead. "Okay," he said finally. "How much can you loan me?"

I put the car in gear and swung around the corner. Motion seemed to clear my head a little. "So where is this place? A filling station?" There was still no traffic, not a car had driven past while we were talking. I cruised along at a walk. He said something I didn't catch. "What? You got an address?" I was feeling better. I was moving, getting someplace.

"Other side of the freeway," he said. "Couple blocks north of University." He had grown quiet, broody.

"Cross on Dale? Western?"

"Huh? Dale, I guess." He wasn't happy, but then the car's acceleration seemed to affect him, too, and without becoming any more cheerful or animated he slid into a kind of mechanical patter. "Knew that old retread was going to blow before it happened, knew it in my guts, but I was just praying it would hold till we got back to Hudson. Traffic-side front, bang, near dragged me into a semi. Big old Peterbilt. Slammed over onto the shoulder to miss it, good thing I know my way behind the wheel. Cop come by, he seen my wife was hurt, so he took her along to the emergency room while I went for a tire. I know this guy who's got one for thirty dollars. That's all I need, thirty dollars, it won't cost you a nickel. The cops, they can take you home, but not if you're from another state. Wish I lived here, I'd already be home." The machinery of his story seemed to run down. He whistled a few bars of something mournful, then turned to me. "You from here? This always been your neighborhood?"

"Yeah," I said, and half waited for Ike's picky correction. I glanced back at him. Strapped like a fighter pilot into a child seat he thought he was too big for, he met my glance with blank seriousness. He had pulled his backpack up onto his lap, and one arm was slipped through the bungee cord that held his sleeping bag rolled. "My wife grew up here," I said. We stopped at a red light. The man was looking around now as if he were searching for a landmark. I looked ahead and saw what I should have thought of before, might have, except that another building still stands there in my mind's eye. "If you're lost, here's the place to get directions." I pointed across University. "Might find your own cop."

I studied the man's rough profile as he looked across the intersection at the beige, blank-faced district police station that had been slapped up against the Lendways Lounge around the time they tore down the Belmont Club, with its "nood lunch" sign. The city had bought out the Belmont and the Notorious Faust porn theater across the street and the nameless little peep shows and porn shops near the corner and pushed the prostitutes a few blocks north, all to make room for respectable businesses that somehow still haven't materialized. Only new business I can think of, if you don't count the police station, is The Exstacy House, four blocks west, selling videos and more.

I had only to cross University, slide in among the shoals of cop cars that I knew were parked behind the temporary-looking station house, and let the rest of it unravel away from me, outside my car, beyond my control. He would get help, social service referral, maybe, or walk away. However it went, it wouldn't matter. I wouldn't have to know. I would say something to Ike about Officer Friendly, drive him to his overnight, then seek out the cozy shelter of a coffee house and let the gray backwash of Thanksgiving evaporate around me.

"I ain't lost," the man said, expressionless. "Turn right here, couple blocks."

"Dad?"

I turned right, drove a block east, past Hong Phat Inc. and Auto

Max, and pulled over to the curb. There was a tire place across the avenue that I had forgotten about, Fred's Tires, big B.F. Goodrich sign. "How about this?" I asked. "They got retreads here."

He didn't even look. "Can't afford a place like that. I don't need just a tire, I need a whole wheel. Cop told me not to drive with that cut tire, it'd wreck the rim. It did, too. Anyway, we got it arranged, guy's going to sell me a used tire and rim."

I felt the warmth of grim confirmation like liquor burning inside me. I couldn't let it go. I needed to move to the end of it, prove something about him and us. Anything less felt unbearable.

"So, where?" I asked, pulling out again into the thin stream of traffic.

"Anywhere along here is fine," he said. "I can walk the rest of the way. I just need the money for that tire." He seemed down and disheartened, as if he were losing hope.

I didn't want him to lose hope. As I kept driving, past the thickening concentrations of Asian businesses, smoke from a kind of low fever seemed to mix intoxicatingly with the man's metallic smell. "We've come this far," I said. "Tell me where to go, we'll see can your guy give you a deal on that tire. Where do I turn? Mackubin? Arundel? Western?"

"Western." I turned north on Western Avenue, and again he said, "Here, this is close enough. I can get off here."

And I suddenly realized with a jolt that he might be scared, some nigger had him in the car and wouldn't let him out. I said, "No, I'll take you all the way."

"Dad," Ike mumbled, working on his tooth again, "we tole Ethan's mom we be there."

"Hang on," I said. "We're almost finished with this." The steering wheel felt like a toy in my grip. I wished that Ike were getting it, how things had swung around. I drove slowly, letting the guy look for his tire seller. "Is this a store we're looking for?" I asked. "Filling station?" He shook his head but said nothing and wouldn't look at me.

Following his muttered, monosyllabic directions, right, left, right again, we were soon beyond the ragged commercial fringe of University Avenue and into a depressing neighborhood of asbestos siding and sagging porches, not just deserted, as our own neighborhood had seemed on a cold, dark afternoon, but abandoned. The rows of houses were gap-toothed, mismatched. This was the slum my father imagined when he thought about where we had moved. Cracked asphalt driveways led past empty foundation sockets overgrown with brush and straggly saplings and bent, frost-burned weeds. One-story development boxes with particle board siding were spliced in between big old wrecks. The trees, where there were trees, looked like they might have been used for hangings.

"Here," he said. "It's right up the alley. You can let me off here." His voice had become dark, out of focus.

There was no alley. I drove around the block and turned east and found a dead-end alley running north and south. "Here?"

"Yeah." He didn't seem to care. I turned down the alley. About halfway into the middle of the block, among back yards that looked like they belonged to some failed industry, not homes where people lived, there was a caved-in garage, with an old Pontiac parked on the gravel and dirt driveway. "Here," the man said without enthusiasm. And then, as an afterthought, "That's the car we're going to get the tire from." He didn't look at it. A wooden telephone pole leaning over the Pontiac's scabby vinyl roof seemed to have been chewed on, in inefficient fury, by some animal with teeth evolved for tearing flesh.

I sat there for a moment behind the wheel, cold dissatisfaction turning slowly in my belly. What had I been expecting? An overalled mechanic shaking my hand? We had come this far. I had obligated myself to put some money into this man's red hands. "Well, you'll need my address, I suppose," I said. Rummaging in the dashboard well, I found a ballpoint and a pencil and an expired Domino's coupon. Free cokes, free twisty breads. I tore the coupon in two and wrote my name and address and phone number on the back of one half while the man wrote on the back of the other.

"I'll give you my work number, too," he said. He was like a machine, his mind working on something else.

We exchanged the torn coupon halves, and I read what he had written, Donny Jimson, and two telephone numbers, one with a 715 area code. "That's Hudson?" I asked. He said it was and got out of the car, leaving the door open.

"I think I'll just stay in the car," Ike said. He wasn't wiggling that tooth anymore. His sleeping bag was piled up against his back pack, you could barely see him, he was so barricaded.

"Sure," I said to him, "this won't take a minute." I hadn't been thinking about getting out of the car, myself, but now it seemed awkward not to. I walked around the car. "So," I said, "where does your man live?" He gestured vaguely to the back of one of the houses, clapboard weathered to bare gray wood, windows puffy with sheets of cloudy plastic frayed and snapping in the hard wind. It must have been left over from last winter, maybe longer. He was waiting. Donny Jimson was waiting for his money. I took out my wallet. "I'll need about forty," he said.

"You said thirty. All along, you're saying thirty."

"Thirty for the tire. I need to get gas, too. Tire's no good to me without gas."

Standing there in the cold wind, sun dropping toward the old roof tops, I felt dizzy, blood pushing too hard behind my eyes. I hadn't gotten anywhere. I was just as certain as ever I was being scammed, just as incapable of saying forget it, turning my back on a man in trouble. I opened the wallet and rummaged a little, trying not to be obvious about how much was in it. We had been paid before Thanksgiving. I took out a ten and a twenty. There was another ten, a five, some ones. I held the thirty dollars in my hand. "You're not going to cheat me, are you?"

"No, man, I'm like you, I'm a Christian. I know what trouble is." He looked down at the bills in my hand. "Couldn't you spare another ten, just to get me home and back? I really need forty."

Standing, he was half a head taller than me, even with his slouch, and younger than I had thought. It was his bad teeth made him look old. Wallet in one hand, ten and twenty in the other, I felt something pulsing angrily, stubbornly, behind my eyes. I said, "I think maybe even thirty is more than enough."

Blood darkened his face. "What is this? Why are you yanking me around this way?"

"Me? Shit, man, you say thirty, then you say forty." I shoved the two bills forward at him. He took them in silence and held them as if they were some spoiled thing. "There," I said. "That's the best I can do for you. I'm really going to need it back before tonight."

He shook his head, his face going purple. "Without gas, what good is the tire?" His arms lifted in a gesture of frustration against the lowering sky.

"Ten dollars buy a lot of gasoline."

"Well," he said, "I need a lot of gasoline."

I stared at his dirty, badly put together face in disbelief and anger, then at the back of the wretched house, now sunk in shadows. "Maybe we should go in and talk with your tire guy," I said. "See can't we get you a better deal, so some be left over for all that gasoline you need."

He looked at me. "Maybe we should."

•

I WAKE BEFORE dawn and get dressed, with just enough light to see Sara's form lying tangled in what might be sleep, but looks nothing like rest. On the way to the bathroom I pass Ike's room, his empty bed, his toys still spread out all over from the mess he and his cousins made there on Thanksgiving Day. He should be downstairs watching television at this hour, cramming in his full allotment of Saturday cartoons. He's not, of course. It's quiet in the living room.

I make coffee, have no appetite for breakfast, try to work in my study. It's still too early to go. They won't have him ready for me. But I have to get out of the house, which is unbalanced and disorienting now, so I walk for a while through the neighborhood.

The house where Sara lived when she was a girl is only a block away from us, though then it was three blocks west of where it stands now. Half the houses on this street were somewhere else, then—big two- and three-story frame houses that were moved when they plowed the interstate through or when they built the Control Data warehouse that now houses a multiplex of three grade schools, or in some other spasm of urban renewal. We enrolled Ike in one of those schools when we moved to the neighborhood. Our house and the really old stone house next to it, pre-Civil War, where there were still ancient apple trees when Sara was little, were here all along, but the next three were uprooted and moved in. The row houses across the street were built about fifteen years ago after they had bulldozed everything on that block, and the Martin Luther King Center is about that old, I guess, and the Lung Association building stands where Sara went to school.

Still, the neighborhood has a settled feel to it, solid, homey. Last year, when I built a fence to protect a bed of irises descended from corms brought north from Missouri by my mother, I built it low, neighborly, so passersby could talk across it comfortably. Some of these satisfactions were in the long, eloquent grace I said on Thanksgiving Day. I can't remember much of it, only isolated, well-turned phrases that now seem thin as eggshells.

I wait till nine o'clock, and then I can't stand it anymore and get into the car. I have to see my son. I'm thinking he won't be ready yet. It's earlier than the time they said they would have him ready. But I have to see him.

We had agreed that I would pick him up around ten. However, he has his pajamas packed and his sleeping bag rolled when I get there, and before we're out the door he whispers, "How did it go?"

"What?"

"You know."

"Yeah."

•

IT WAS THIRTY-THREE dollars, in the end. While I was hesitating, Ike had called to me from the car, "Dad, I have to pee!" and I gave it up. I gave the man the three ones from my wallet and said, "That's got to be it," and he turned and walked away, past the house, heading west when I lost sight of him. On the way to his friend's house finally, Ike asked me was the man going to give me the money back, and I said I didn't know. Maybe not. Ike said he thought the man wouldn't.

·

"I GUESS HE scammed me," I admit now, as Ike dumps his stuff into the back seat. "You were right. He hasn't brought the money back."

And Ike finally breaks down. He cries out, "I told you! He was ugly. He could have hurt me. Couldn't you see how he looked?"

"He was furious with me," I tell Sara after we've put Ike to bed, and add hastily, "as he had every right to be." The house is no longer heeled over sickeningly by the shadow of disaster, though we have a ways to go before we can rest comfortably. What nags at me is that, even knowing how justified he was, how dangerous my niggling stubbornness had been for both of us, I couldn't help trying to correct him. Said, "You can't judge somebody bad for being ugly or wearing bad clothes." And he just shouted at me, "I know that. Everybody knows that." So I shut up then. "I'm just glad he didn't see it as a race thing," I tell her. "It wasn't a race thing."

"That so?" Then Sara is silent for a long time, a silence I brace my heart against. Finally she speaks. She says to me, "You're a good man. You can't help that. Otherwise, you wouldn't be in my house, don't mention in my bed. But you, by God, cannot afford to be a fool. None of us so prosperous we can afford that. Not in this world. Not in this country. None of us."

FEAST OF THE CIRCUMCISION

When my father lost his testicles, I was in Germany, but I was back home in St. Paul and available to drive him to the mall when he needed to be circumcised. His penis kept getting irritated and enflamed after the orchiectomy, my mother told me as I unpacked in my old bedroom. They thought it had to do with loss of hormones, she said. Or maybe it was the estrogen therapy, intended to inhibit further spread of the prostate cancer.

I didn't encourage her to talk about it; the less I knew, the happier I was. But she stood in the doorway, rattling on, laying medical information on me as if I could use it to save his life. She had a new haircut, a stylish wedge in place of the wavy cascade that had fallen to the middle of her back for as long as I could remember, and every once in a while she touched it automatically, fingering its slope, still not used to it. "You understand?" she asked, about what in particular I had no idea. I nodded, slid a dresser drawer shut, turned around, and saw the expression on her face. She really did expect me to save his life.

We left the house early in the morning, without a decent breakfast. Because of my father's high cholesterol, my parents had started eating fibery cold cereal for breakfast, who always used to celebrate my homecomings with waffles and bacon and eggs and hash browns. As we pulled away from the house, I could see through the kitchen window my mother standing at the sink, looking out, watching us, I assumed. She had never learned to drive, though recently she had started to talk about it again, Driver's Ed at sixty years old.

We drove in silence. Like my father, I had been spared the routine circumcision still inflicted on most American baby boys, and I was shaken by the thought of having it done as an adult. It was nothing compared to the operation that had preceded it, but I hadn't been around for that one. I had been overseas, preoccupied with problems of my own, and the horror hadn't really sunk in. It was sinking in now.

Slumped beside me in my rented Audi, staring straight ahead rather than jabbing his finger at this or that danger bearing down on us, this or that pedestrian I might have killed, my father appeared passive, stoical. He taught philosophy at a Catholic women's college in St. Paul, but he was far from being a philosophical man, and this quiet resignation was unsettling to me. When I was a kid, he had been given to violent rages over my least mistake, my slightest lapse in judgment. Later, after I had discovered a gift for statistical analysis and went from educational misfit to academic star, he would still argue with me stubbornly about every decision I made. He certainly would not have been able to understand the mess I had left behind in Freiburg, where I had been doing research on the EEU and having an affair with a senior colleague's irresistible wife. My father had gone berserk over a briefly pregnant girlfriend when I was in college—what would he say about Erik's attempted suicide after the blow-up, or Ilsa's expecting me to move in with her and their nine-year-old daughter?

In the matter of his own rebelling body, however, my father seemed to have achieved a bizarre acceptance. He wasn't slumped down in the seat, I realized—he was shrunken, he was barely there anymore. That was maybe what my mother had meant when she had called me in Germany and told me I needed to come home. I had welcomed the excuse to leave, and I thought I was properly braced for the end. Only now, however, was I beginning to feel loss easing its actual and outrageous knife into my heart. In a coffin, he would have been adjusted, corrected, restored. He would have been made to look something like his real self. He would have been my father again, though dead.

The clinic was a generic suite of offices in a suburban strip mall, State Farm agency on one side, Footlocker on the other. Mauve and gray waiting room, a dozen or so leatherette chairs. Curved, formica reception desk, behind which a beautiful, Hispanic-looking receptionist, long hair drawn back into a thick, sleek braid, was working on her nails.

We arrived thirty minutes before the procedure was scheduled, but the room was already half filled, and we had to settle for seats on opposite sides of a towering fish tank flickering occasionally with a glance of brilliant tropical fish. Distorted by the octagonal tank, my father's jowly face and bald head, fringed with still-dark curls, appeared to hang suspended in the water, something from the depths beyond sunlight, bulgy-eyed and massive. But when I leaned forward to say something to him, the man I saw was drained and faded and negligible. I sat back again, feeling abandoned, unfairly punished.

Patients continued to check in after us, until the room was filled with people bundled against the cold March weather. Most of them were old. They left their coats on and sat thumbing magazines or talking in brief, unhappy bursts or just staring ahead of them. After our scheduled time had passed, I went up to the reception desk, at first to flirt a little with the receptionist, who had a misleadingly open, inviting face, then to express my growing irritation about the long wait. After a while she wouldn't even look at me, scanned the room as if there were something there that deserved her attention, if only I would quit bothering her.

After an hour and a half, when my father's name had still not been called, I was startled from a stupor of hunger and boredom by the smack of an old *Discover* magazine he apparently had slammed down on the glass coffee table, with enough force that everyone in the waiting room looked up, including the chilly receptionist. This was more like it. This was the father I remembered. Encouraged, I went up to the reception desk, and, as before, the receptionist wouldn't condescend to make eye contact, repeating to the air next to my head that they were doing all that they could, there had been an emergency, everyone had to have understanding. That's how she put it, "We have to have understanding." I could smell the heavy musk of her perfume, but otherwise it was as if she sat behind bulletproof glass.

Oh, I had understanding. I returned to my father and said, "Okay, that's it, let's go." But he just shrugged and waved me back to my chair. Maybe he hadn't meant to slam the magazine down. Maybe it had just slipped out of his weakened fingers.

Finally, a middle-aged nurse came out and ushered him away through one of the waiting room's three doors. A pathetic sight. It didn't seem possible that this vague man had once been so monumental, such an infuriating antagonist. I reminded myself that after forty years of teaching he was still an assistant professor, having never finished his Ph.D., tenured only by inertia. A Swedish Lutheran farm boy in an Irish Catholic college, he had never lost the outsider's edgy, self-defeating wariness. He had never acquired academic polish, never had the ambition to publish. But he had always seemed enormously powerful to me. And now he was being led off to have a baby's operation, a cultic ritual from somebody else's cult.

I studied a photograph of an intricately-chipped Maya flint in a *National Geographic* and thought about Ilsa, my lover in Germany. She had known what to do with a foreskin. The first time we had sex, I complimented her on it, and she remarked that she had never made love with any but uncircumcised men. At the time I had felt part of a privileged club, but I wondered now whether there had been something anti-Semitic in the comment. Her politics were liberal enough, but when things had started to get ugly between her and poor old Erik, her ruthlessness gave me the willies.

After a while, a white-coated doctor about my own age came out and asked if my father typically had problems with high blood pressure. Only when something upset him, I said. He had been made to wait over two hours—of course his blood pressure was up. Later, I remembered my mother talking about the hypertension medicine he had been taking for years, but I was sure that this time it was circumstantial.

"We'll have to wait for it to go down," the doctor said.

"Waiting is what cranked it up there in the first place. How do you figure more waiting will bring it down?"

"We've given him a tranquilizer."

Give me one, I thought, as I returned to the magazine. Prostate cancer was in my own cards, I was mournfully sure of that. It ran in the family. I found myself compulsively visualizing the stupidly designed organ that evolution had strangled around our innocent urethras. Sixty-four years old. My father was not old enough to be so far gone. I shifted uncomfortably in the chair and turned to an advertisement for beef—real food for real people.

Although it was only about eleven o'clock, I had been thinking for some time about places on the strip where we might stop to eat on the way home. I have never outgrown the pleasure restaurant meals with my parents gave me as a child, the sense of entitlement, membership in the adult world where you asked for something and they brought it to you. At thirty-two, I had lived in some of the greatest cities of Europe. I had been married for a while to a graduate of the Sorbonne, a gourmet cook. Yet the prospect of lunch with my father at Embers or Appleby's absurdly pleased me. And then I had an inspiration.

I checked my watch. You would think they were doing a coronary bypass. Finally, my father shuffled out into the waiting area, did a little paperwork at the desk, and told me to get him out of there.

"How do you feel?" I asked.

"Sore." He leaned on my arm as we walked to the elevator, an unaccustomed intimacy, and agreed with neither enthusiasm nor reluctance that we could stop somewhere for lunch. It was appalling, his lack of interest, his refusal to assert himself.

Instead of stopping at one of the highway restaurants, I drove all the way back into St. Paul, back into our own neighborhood, which had been rough when I was a kid growing up—breaking windows, getting into fights, desperate to prove that I was as tough as anybody I ran with. The neighborhood had turned around since I had left home, and now the business area a few blocks from our house was filled with restaurants.

"There's a new place on Selby I saw when I was driving in from the airport," I said. "Not far from you. Maybe you and Mom have been there."

I knew they hadn't. She might have, if a friend went with her, but he would have thought it a crazy extravagance to pay for a restaurant meal within walking distance of his own kitchen, his own wife's reliable cooking.

He slumped beside me in the passenger seat, staring ahead at nothing for a while. Then he said, "Remember when Selby was nothing but bars." I couldn't tell if it was a question or a declaration. He spoke in a tight, wary manner, as if it were his tongue that had been clipped.

"You'll like this place," I said. "It's perfect." I parked in front and helped him out of the car. He moved gingerly, absorbed in his discomfort, head bent like somebody lugging a cross, and I wondered how long it would take him to notice, to get the little joke. I couldn't tell if he registered the name painted onto the window, Old Jerusalem Café. When we stepped in the door, the warm rush of garlic seemed to straighten him up a little, but even when a waitress had seated us at one of the wooden tables and he had the kosher vegetarian menu spread open in front of him, he said nothing.

Only after the waitress came back and took our orders did he look at me. "Very funny."

"You've been initiated," I said. "Mazel tov!"

"Very funny," he said again, but this time I was surprised to see that he maybe did think it was funny. I looked around. It wasn't noon yet, but the restaurant was loud with voices, the deli counter in back stood three or four deep in waiting customers, and most of the tables were filled. Not an especially Jewish-seeming crowd, the usual neighborhood mix, but there was a Hasidic family that would never have been seen around there when I was a kid, and our waitress had that ravishing Middle Eastern generosity of hair and face and figure. When she came to refill our coffee cups, she rested a hand familiarly on my father's shoulder.

"And how are you gentlemen doing today?" A little bit of an accent, just a trace, enough to tickle a little in your ear.

"You wouldn't believe it," I said. But she wasn't listening to me—she was telling my father something I couldn't make out in the din. I felt my face grow hot, and I told myself it was for my mother, eating her chicken salad sandwich or something a few blocks away. We were her whole life. After the waitress left, I asked, "Well, Dad, how are you doing?"

"You wouldn't believe it."

I couldn't read his expression. When he drew in like that, it was usually a trap, liable to hurt me before long. I pushed on, though. "It must be awful."

He shrugged.

"Cancer," I said. "The surgery."

"It's been no picnic."

"I can't imagine what you've gone through." I had tried hard not to. In the moist, fragrant heat of the restaurant, I felt like a foreigner. "The operation. How do you feel about it now?"

"Sore, like I told you. Sore as hell."

"Not the circumcision." How did therapists do it? I felt like shaking him. "How do you deal with it, what's happened?"

He was looking around, as if searching for someone he knew, before turning back to me. "Frankie, tell you a story. True story. When I was in for the operation, the big one, I got to know one of the nurses pretty well." He stopped, and I struggled to think of something to say, but then he got going again. "We'd joke around. Humorous girl, pretty direct, and once we were talking about the medical term, orchiectomy, how it sounds like something with flowers, and she said they had had a guy in there once, foundry worker—six-four, six-five—big, muscular guy. He was in for an orchiectomy like me, and he seemed awfully calm about it. She wondered if maybe he wasn't clear about the operation and so she asked him, Mister whoever it was, had the doctor explained what they were going to do? And he said, 'Sure. They're going to take out my intestes.' And she said, 'Your testes.' He shrugs, he doesn't care how they pronounce it. And she says again, 'Testes. Testicles.' He still looks blank. Finally she says, 'Your nuts. They're going to cut off your nuts.' And the poor guy faints dead away. He'd had no idea."

I gave a shocked laugh. "Some story to tell a man in your situation."

"No, I appreciated it. A fellow your age thinks it would be worse than death, but believe me, it isn't. Your mother still loves me, I still have to shave. My doctor even told me it's possible to have sex, though I don't think so. I'm just glad to be alive. I'm still a father. I'm still a man."

He drank some coffee, and the waitress arrived with our meals: a pita sandwich for me, and for him a plate of some sort of ratatouille and big, gray knishes and a salad full of olives and rings of red onion. She touched him again, running her hand across the back of his faded old suit coat so lightly that he might not have noticed.

"Still," I said, "it's not professional, telling you that sort of story." It was so much stronger than any snap-out-of-it slap I had thought to offer him, I felt it stinging on my own cheek.

"I think she was doing what you've been doing here, Frankie."

I looked at him.

"She was showing me she knew I could take it. Bad as it was, I could take it. I could even laugh at it."

I stared down at my plate, willing to embrace that interpretation, for her, for myself. He began to eat his ratatouille thing, with more energy than I had seen him display since I had returned home. Okay, I thought, I give up. If acceptance can go this far, effect such a transformation of character, I'll bow my head to it. I'll embrace it with gratitude.

"Dad," I said, after a long silence, "there's this woman I've been seeing in Germany," and began unraveling the tangled thread that trailed between Freiburg and me, between Ilsa and Erik and me.

He put his fork down as I spoke. His loose, gray face slowly surged with blood. There he was, I realized, for the first time since I had come home from Germany, my father. My old father, filled with anger and disappointment and righteous judgment, was back.

RUN

WHETHER YOU SAW it or only heard the noise depended on which way you were facing, it happened that fast. A hot summer evening had drawn everyone in our leafy urban neighborhood out of doors. My kids, Hannah and Willy, were on the sidewalk in front of the house, horsing around with the hose while I gathered up sponges and rags and buckets from the curb. They had been helping me wash the car, and we were all in our swimsuits. Ike, Willy's fifth grade classmate from next door, had just run out with a Super Soaker to join the water fight, and his parents, Isaiah and Sara, were on their front porch painting the wooden spindles of its intricate Victorian gingerbread. Rita Vogel was talking with them from the sidewalk, not minding the occasional bursts of hose spray that shot her way, though I warned the kids to watch it. Farther down the block, Mr. Grosz was edging his lawn, and on the public courts in the park across the street the tennis players had switched to doubles, and even so the benches were filled with waiting players.

The air was rich with the luxurious pock, pock, pock of tennis balls and laughter and the fragrance of spraying water when a squeal of tires exploded from the side street thirty feet away, a speeding car trying to make the corner, skidding at the T of the intersection, shrieking sideways, a screaming of engine and tires and catastrophe, managing the turn somehow, wildly swerving the other way, smashing into my gleaming black Crown Victoria so hard the heavy car bucked and heaved up over the curb. The impact knocked loose a chunk of granite curb as big as a man's shoe and flung it onto the sidewalk, missing Hannah by inches, and my car landed groaning, shuddering with two wheels up on the boulevard.

The green junker came to a thunderous stop, mashed up against my car. The driver sat there a second, as stunned as all of us were, then, before the rest of us came back to life, he shouted something, and a boy about ten years old leaped out the passenger side door and took off, and the driver, maybe eighteen, piled out after him, both of them tearing away through the park.

And though I felt I was still standing there in front of my house with my neighbors and children, frozen, I found myself in motion, pursuing them, barefoot, wearing swimming trunks, tank top, and baseball cap, blasting across the street and onto the slippery, child-beaten grass of the park, driven by reflex as purely as if I had been launched from a catapult. As I passed the tall chain-link fence of the tennis courts, I was half-conscious of the players, transfixed, a blur of black faces and white shirts, then I was pounding up the hill beyond the courts to the sidewalk running between the school and the community center, a straightaway where I thought I was starting to gain on them.

The guy who had been driving had caught up with the boy by now. The boy glanced up at him as he passed, but the guy just swerved onto the weedy ground for a few paces and then hit the concrete sidewalk again and raced on, his dark skin flashing where the wind of his own speed lifted the open shirt from his back, the boy lunging after him as if he could be carried along by the yellow cloth streaming ahead of him. On the boy's thin body, a striped T-shirt rippled and twisted above baggy jeans.

The slapping of our feet against the sidewalk echoed between blank walls. When the driver and then the boy shot out of shadow into the evening sun beyond the buildings, they seemed fixed for a moment, held by the light, and I bore down on them, reeling in the distance separating us until I, too, burst into the sun again and the three of us, evenly spaced now, raced past the school's jungle gym, swings, and slide, across the hot, soft asphalt playground onto the field that stretched away toward a distant purr of traffic.

The field was in chaos, a work in progress. From the beginning of summer, massive tractors had been pulling disk harrows back and forth, ripping open the inner city earth. Day after day a front end loader on clanking tracks had been scraping and scooping up the soil and dumping it into a huge steel cube that stood in the middle of the field and shook violently for hours, separating rocks from dirt.

The monstrous earth-movers and rock-sifter stood silent in the field now, abandoned in the distance. By the time the boy reached the low, black fabric silt fence that surrounded the plowed territory, the driver was half way across the field. I wasn't going to catch him, but I was close enough to the boy to hear his thin breath rasping in his throat. He was lighter-skinned than the driver, with hair the color of cinnamon. I lunged and grabbed at him as he jumped the taut nylon fabric into the plowed field, then I stumbled crossing it myself and fell back a few yards before regaining my balance.

The boy leaped ahead of me like a rabbit, dodging from side to side as he made his way over the torn-up, treacherous ground. It was heavy going for both of us. The earth was cold and sticky underfoot, slippery with streaks of greenish clay, impossible to gain real traction. My bare feet sank in past the ankles sometimes, and sometimes scraped against rocks that had not yet been uprooted and sifted from the dirt. The raw soil reeked of swamp, as if there had been an ancient lake bed here, and that was why the land stood empty still, surrounded by the city.

My side ached. The driver was out of sight. The boy dodged through a gate in the chain-link fence on the far side of the field, dropped down a steep bank toward the avenue, and plunged without hesitation into a stream of traffic. Half way across he was struck by the roar of a truck's diesel horn and staggered to a momentary stop before racing ahead again. I timed the flow of cars and made it across the street a dozen steps behind him. He ran across a vacant lot behind the Lutheran Church, through the back yards of brick apartment buildings and old frame houses, into a neighborhood of gnarled, woody hedges of lilac and spirea overhanging the sidewalk that lashed at me as I ran past, elephant-eared catalpa trees in the boulevard twisting around wounds where limbs had been torn away.

My own neighborhood a few blocks away was an old one, too, its houses dating from the turn of the century and one from before the Civil War, but this was different. The years hung in the air here like smoke, clinging to every surface. The smooth roots of trees heaved out of the packed dust as I blurred over them, thinking I remembered another slum-clearance park being here, with a sloping, misaligned, unplayable tennis court and everything built of poured concrete from the fortress days of urban renewal twenty or thirty years ago—a basketball court with monumental concrete standard, concrete picnic tables, concrete benches, everything massive as machine gun bunkers. But where I was running now there were only streets of houses weathered free of paint, shingles cupped and mossy, and in the alleys, two-story garages with haymows and swinging doors settled deep into the earth.

We had taken some turn—I didn't know where I was anymore but couldn't stop to get my bearings. The boy led me down alleys where cobblestones struck against my bare heels like sledgehammers, through yards choked with gardens, shaded by houses built close enough together to cast a chill.

I finally caught the boy in a side yard as he was trying to scale a stockade fence, gray and rotting, that surrounded an old brownstone mansion. I grabbed him by the back of his shirt, heard a seam tear, wrestled him to the ground, straddled him while he writhed and cursed. Then he went still, only his narrow chest heaving, his teeth clenched in a grimace.

I looked up and saw a group of black people coming toward us. "Hey," I shouted to them, "somebody call the cops." They gathered around us, kids running up first, then some women, then more kids and some men. "You need to call the police," I said. "This boy's been involved in an accident."

They looked down at us. I debated getting off, but the boy would slip free if I wasn't sitting on him. Both of us were slick with mud and sweat. I was conscious of my stink, and of a sharp pain pulsing in the ball of my right foot. I must have cut it on something. "Looks to me like you're the accident," a large woman said, and somebody laughed.

A little girl, who couldn't have been older than five or six, stepped forward. "What's the matter with you?" she asked. "Why you sitting on him like that?" The question surged and reverberated through the group, which was getting larger. I couldn't tell from my position on the ground how many adults and children there were, but together they seemed to fill the space between the fence and the next house.

"I think you best leave that boy stand up," somebody said, and the kids shrieked like terrible amplifiers.

"Let him go, you son of a bitch!" the little girl screamed.

"Keesha!"

The girl dodged out of the large woman's reach and circled around to the other side of me. "You should be ashamed!" she shouted at me.

I *was* ashamed, kneeling there over that boy, the sun glaring against my pink scalp and shoulders and filthy legs. I felt dizzy. Some of the people surrounding me might have been on their way to church service, the women in nice dresses, the men in dark trousers and white shirts.

An old woman stepped forward. She was tall. I could barely see her face against the evening sun. Her gray hair was pulled back tightly and fastened somehow in back. She said, "You get on up now." It seemed to me that she was talking to the boy, but I got up and helped the boy to his feet.

"Let loose of his arm," the old woman said. Even standing, I was shorter than she. "Let loose now," she said again.

I unclenched my fist from around his upper arm, thin and hard as the handle of a baseball bat. He rubbed the place where I had been holding him.

"There was an accident," I said once more. "You maybe saw the driver run through here. This boy was in the car. He might have been hurt."

"Anybody hurt him—" the large woman started to say. Then she reached over and scooped him toward her, gathered him to her soft, abundant front for a moment, heedless of the dirt on him. "You okay, baby?"

"It's not him," I said. "It's the guy who was driving—he left the scene of an accident. I don't know, maybe he was drinking. Is that why he ran?" I asked the boy.

"You just be let him be," the large woman said. The boy looked away. A police siren rose and fell, coming nearer.

"They'll want to talk with him," I said, "get that driver's name. Did somebody call them?" The siren breathed in and out, diminishing after a minute or so, falling silent.

"Look," the little girl said, pointing at my foot, "he bleeding."

I lifted my foot from the sticky grass. A man stepped forward and took my arm, supporting me, while the large woman bent over and lifted my filthy leg, cradling my foot in her warm, smooth hand, turning it so the blood trickled along the base of my toes, thinning the muck that clung there. The tall, gray-haired woman reached into her purse and handed the large woman a crisply folded cotton handkerchief. She touched it to the ball of my foot. "That hurt?"

"Not bad."

"You got to go wash that out good, put on some iodine." She flipped the handkerchief into a long roll and looped it around my foot and tied it on top with a tight, tiny knot . "Help a little," she said. "There's glass all over the place. You got to be crazy, running around barefoot."

A white policeman came around the side of a house. I could see his squad car parked out on the street. "You the guy whose car got hit?" he asked.

I looked around. The boy was gone. The young man who had been helping me balance on one foot let me lean on him as I hobbled out to the street. I tried not to get his shirt dirty. The cop reached to open the passenger side door of the cruiser, but I had already started to get into the back. The little girl handed me my cap.

"Thank you," I said. She glared at me.

The cop didn't say anything to me for a block or so, talking cryptically on the radio. Then he looked at me in the rearview mirror. A wire grill separated us. "Got away, huh?"

"Yeah."

"Well, don't feel bad. They run like the wind."

When we turned onto my block, I could see another squad car pulled up behind the violently coupled wreckage, and a cop taking a statement from Isaiah. Rita and Sara were standing on the boulevard a little farther on, and Hannah, Willy, and Ike were peering into the green junker's windows. I knew their names. They were my neighbors, my children. I remembered them from another life.

WHAT IS *SON*?

THIS IS MY cathedral, she says in Spanish, sweeping her hands wide to embrace the tenement rooftop, the wire clotheslines strung overhead from canted, rusting poles, the ponderous dome of tropical night sky. She is María Haidí, the Afro Cuban woman who is going to teach these Lutheran pastors and professors and college administrators to dance in Old Havana. From a corner of the roof, a tower and part of the façade of Havana's baroque cathedral a few blocks away is visible, though the visitors are so disoriented still from their first day in Cuba that they barely get her joke. María Haidí opens her palms to the spidery tangles of two television antennas, one strapped at its base to a crumbling brick chimney, the other screwed to the little shed at the top of the dizzyingly steep stairway that had led them up here: These are my bell towers, she says. Welcome.

There are fifteen of them in the delegation from St. Paul, Minnesota, U.S.A., eight men and seven women, seated in folding chairs on the roof in a ragged semicircle. Tom Vogel had grabbed one of the chairs farthest from the cleared space in the center of the roof, where María Haidí is beginning to explain the essence of Cuban music, which she says is the essence of Cuba, and the instruments, and the rhythms, while their tour leader translates into English and three other Cubans—musicians, apparently—stand around behind her and periodically hand her instruments—ebony claves, maracas, a little drum, a ridged gourd rasped with a stick, a bead-encrusted rattle the size of a watermelon—or step forward themselves to demonstrate. The tres with its three doubled strings. A waist-high conga drum.

The band members may be members of her family, though none is nearly as black as she is, whose skin is the color of a freshly-blued

111

gun barrel. A wiry, gray-haired man may be her husband, a teenaged girl in spandex shorts may be her granddaughter. María Haidí's long print dress sways over her ankles and bare feet as she sails through her lecture, clinking the claves against each other in various complicated rhythmic variations, singing scraps of melody.

The musicians take up instruments, and the group plays a guajira, traditional country music, then something salsa, then something else. And *son*? What is *son*, again? Tom wonders. It's confusing but pretty in the soft January night atop a decaying colonial palacio, and when a little girl comes out and hands everyone slender paper cones full of peanuts, and an older girl serves mojitos in plastic glasses from a rusty cookie sheet, and Jorge, the tour leader, translates the gist of María Haidí's sweet, sly jokes, it is easy to forget that something scary is inexorably sweeping toward them.

Tom Vogel cannot be the only one braced behind a mask of laughter and applause and tipsy appreciation. These aren't the first mojitos they have been served today. During one of the songs, a beautiful young man and woman slipped out of the stairway shed and are perched now on the rooftop's wall like cats. Tom edges his chair back a little to get a better look past the thick, bobbing shoulders of Jack Olson, the college chaplain, who arranged the Cuba trip. And suddenly he feels himself toppling backward toward the empty night air and the cobblestone street three long stories below. Before he has a chance to cry out, a stone balustrade catches him, stops his fall. It holds him there, the rear legs of his chair sunk in a kind of gutter, staring up at the dim stars and unnaturally horizontal sliver of moon.

Heart banging in his chest, he stays that way for a minute, tilted back as if he could not be more comfortable. Half of his mojito sloshed out, but most of it ended up on the tar and concrete roof rather than on his trousers. He sips the sweet, watery drink. The young man is watching him from across the rooftop. No one else seems to have noticed the incident. The young man leans over and says something to the young woman beside him, the music crashes to a close, and the audience applauds.

The young man and the young woman come forward, and María Haidí introduces them, Roberto and Isabel, who will demonstrate some of the dances of Cuba. The little band plays, Roberto takes Isabel in his arms, and they dance beneath the yellow light of a few bare bulbs, twining as effortlessly as if they were one being, the two of them and the music, salsa or meringue (or *son*, what was that?), and they occupy the complicated rhythms so completely it is hopeless to parse the movements of their feet. Tom gives up trying. Isabel is wearing a little tank top and a short skirt that swirls above her muscular legs. Roberto's seafoam guayabera shirt is open to the middle of his smooth brown chest, and his tight black pants shimmer like streams of oil pouring over his tireless thighs and calves and ankles.

"Cute," Denise Albrecht murmurs in Tom's direction without taking her eyes off the dancers. Tom returns his chair to level, drags the back legs out of the gutter, and leans forward to hear what she is saying: "They are such a cute couple." She is a professor of Old Testament studies at the college, where Tom taught a social theology course last semester.

"Very cute," he says. But they are not a couple, he's pretty sure. Except in the dance. Passionately together as the music spins them, their bodies swirling into each other, lips wet and drawn, he senses a fine fabric of reserve stretched invisibly between them. "Gorgeous," Tom says, when it seems as if Denise is waiting for something else from him, and he applauds with the others as the dance ends and the beautiful girl embraces the beautiful boy. Hot, hot, yet they are not into each other, he is sure of it, and for a second, as the dancers are bowing and pretending to catch their breath, Roberto meets his eyes.

Son—she is saying something about *son* again. Doesn't it just mean "sound"? María Haidí shows them in slow motion the steps of some dance, the basis of all the others, she says, her fine-boned feet swirling like trout beneath the hem of her dress, which she lifts so everyone can see. Like this and this and this. Like this and this and this and then this. And then a variation, then another. Tom feels the muscles of his face quiver with the exhaustion of too much smiling, too much feigned interest and appreciation as the little grupo begins another song. Really, he doesn't care about Cuban music one way or another, though he knows he should love it, everybody loves it. And dance has always been a realm of inadequacy and embarrassment for him.

Roberto and Isabel move into the center of the audience square in each other arms, whirl and dance. And then Isabel is drawing a red-faced, laughing sociologist to his feet, Steve Amos, the only man in the tour group relaxed or clueless enough to wear shorts to this evening program in Old Havana, and she leads him into the salsa steps. He's pretty good, and Roberto coaxes Julie Lux onto the dance floor, the dean of women, and then puts Steve and Julie together, and two others, and two others, with great applause and nervous laughter from those still sitting, until the end of the song.

María Haidí shows them another dance step, Roberto and Isabel demonstrate it, but this time they leave the Lutherans seated, though Steve and several others who were drawn into the previous dance are jumping around in their chairs, agitating to be included. After another dance is explained and the musicians begin to play, Isabel and Roberto go to the newly-experienced dancers, dance with them a little, pair them up, pull others to their feet, some protesting lamely but obviously pleased to be included.

The group is dividing comfortably into dancers and spectators, the spectators careful to show what a good time they are having without drawing attention to themselves. Tom feels himself relax in the soft purr of rum and sugar and tropical breeze off Havana harbor and the satisfaction that he has actually gotten to Cuba, tagging along with this delegation whose mission isn't remotely clear to him. It's not political, they have been told that often enough. They are mostly left-leaning in their own minds, sympathetic to the Revolution in a Lutheran, non-activist way. Dave Reinhart from Business Administration and Rachel Weeks from Philosophy are unabashed capitalists, and that seems fine, too. A goodwill trip. People to people. Witness, one of their orientation speakers had said, but Jack was quick to clarify that it wasn't witness in the Lutheran sense, evangelism. Tom doesn't know what it means, but he is still tingling with the luck of having been included, after such a short time at the college. Cuba. Here he is in Cuba, on the rooftop of a decaying colonial building in Old Havana in January, 1999, learning to dance.

Learning to dance: that's the rub. The boundary between dancers and spectators inexorably deteriorates as Roberto and Isabel invade the realm of the wallflowers, pulling more and more Lutherans onto the dance floor, guiding them through the elementary steps, pairing them up when they seem to have it, moving on relentlessly. Roberto grabs Irene MacDougal, lucky woman, Political Science, and Tom thinks he has one more song to go and might even escape unscathed, there are more men than women and the pairing is resolutely heterosexual, when suddenly Isabel is standing in front of him and taking him by both hands and guiding him into the awkwardly bumping herd of pastors and professors and academic administrators.

She places his hands here and here, she counts the beats for him in practiced English, she holds him close enough to her lean body that he moves automatically with her, with the music (*Son?* Is this *son?*), and it's as effortless as flying is in dreams, he's dancing. And she looks up at him and murmurs the other English phrase she must have memorized long ago, "You dance very well!" And with that it all falls apart, he misses the beat, almost stumbles her into another couple, and they struggle through the rest of the endless song. "Okay!" she says, "Bueno!" and lets him and the others sit down as she and Roberto demonstrate something unbelievably fast and complicated, clearly a virtuoso dance, no threat to the Lutherans from St. Paul.

The evening slides on that way, demonstrations of dizzyingly difficult dances by the professionals, easier dances in which the visitors participate. The Lutherans have settled back into their chairs, pleased with themselves, even the most clumsy, proud of having taken part, when María Haidí steps forward with Jorge interpreting and says that this next dance, the guaguanco, is a very erotic one, in which the man tries to touch the woman's sex and she tries to keep him from doing so. She evades him, María Haidí says, but she doesn't make him go away. The band plays, and Roberto and Isabel begin what seems an ordinary rumba. Then Isabel whirls away and Roberto pursues her, indeed feinting toward her crotch with thrusts of his hips, his hands, his tight buttocks, while Isabel dodges away, never missing a step, never letting him touch her there, never making him go away. He uses a napkin sometimes, María Haidí says, and Roberto pulls a big silk handkerchief out of his pocket and flicks it toward his partner's sex, and sometimes the woman does, too, she says, and Isabel grabs a handkerchief of her own from one of the musicians and waves it toward Roberto, evading, inviting.

The Lutherans are laughing in disbelief, some of them applauding, good sports or good anthropologists or just red-blooded, tolerant Minnesotans. Tom studies Roberto's face whenever he gets a glance of it, trying to read his expression. He has a funny thought and leans over to Denise and asks, "Do you suppose we'll get a chance to try this one?"

And as soon as the sentence is out of his mouth, Denise laughing appreciatively at his joke, Isabel is drawing Steve from the row in front of him, and clueless or cool, grinning, blond, red-faced Steve attempts some version of the rumba steps and makes tentative gestures with his hands towards Isabel's midriff, not an inch lower, while she keeps her distance and pretends to be fending him off. Then she pulls Irene to her feet—really pulls her—and parks her on the dance floor in front of Steve, and then gets Jack onto the floor with herself and waves her handkerchief in his red face framed by that snow-white Hemingway beard, then others and others, until Tom finds himself with all the rest of them out on the tarred rooftop dance floor, chugging around in the throes of some kind of waking dream, no longer worrying about their feet or the beat or what *son* is. Those who have scarves or handkerchiefs pull them out of pockets, flick away, witnessing what they can't quite believe and will never be able to explain.

It doesn't matter how many men or women there are now, since most of them are avoiding a too-obvious couple-dance anyway. Tom finds himself close to Roberto and keeps an eye on him while going through the motions of erotic pursuit with Denise and Linda Prochnow, the chair of foreign languages, who have let him into a kind of friendly triangle. Roberto is swaying and gyrating in front of Barbara Beckmeister, from English, who is grinning and grabbing for him in a manner that is clearly confusing him, though he hangs in there. She isn't grinning, Tom realizes. It's a grimace of indignation. She really is angry, she would knee him if she could, double him over his genitals, if he weren't so agile. Had he actually touched her? Tom is edging his point of the triangle between them, as if by accident, when the song ends, leaving the Lutherans giddy with their own naughtiness.

María Haidí is laughing and clapping in admiration, she can't believe it, they're the best group ever. When they have settled themselves back in their chairs, she explains more dances. Roberto and Isabel demonstrate, the little band plays, the Lutherans dance or stand around talking or sit it out, nobody is paying attention any more. The little girl and Isabel appear with cassette tapes cheaply labeled "*María Haidí y Son de Cuba*," and they sell out, at five dollars apiece. Roberto has disappeared.

On the bus back to the hotel afterwards, Denise drops into the seat next to Tom. "Whew!" she says.

"Whew. You said it." Tom doesn't know her very well. Though they teach in the same department, he is just a part-timer.

She leans in close to him. "Did you see Jack and that girl at the end?"

"Isabel?"

"He was like a grizzly bear, hugging the poor little thing." She half stands up in the seat. "Hey, Jack!" He must have been somewhere near the front of the darkened bus and doesn't respond. Denise sinks back into the seat. "He told me she called him 'Papa,' because he looks like Hemingway. I've never seen him so pleased with himself."

"He does, sort of."

"I told him, 'Watch out for Roberto afterwards. He saw you pawing his partner.'"

"I don't think they're actually a couple," Tom says.

She digs around in her purse, looking for something. "They're brother and sister," she says.

"What?"

"I was talking with one of the musicians."

"Well, I thought it was something like that."

"Imagine him dancing with a partner who's *not* his sister!"

"I better not."

Denise laughs. "*You'd* better not? Whew!"

"Whew," he says, "you said it."

And in the dark night they cruise along the Malecón, the sea on one side and ruined old buildings on the other, columned, porticoed, balconied, louvered, their pastel paint long ago weathered into ghosts of color. What is *son*, exactly? he thinks of asking her, but instead turns the other way and stares out the window at the glittering waters of Havana harbor, the lights of terrible Moro Castle shining in the distance, the bright finger of a lighthouse searching.

MY WASPS

Before the Mexicans tore off our roof, I would sometimes find golf-ball-sized wasp nests hanging like tiny piñatas under the eaves when I crawled up there in late autumn or early spring to muck out the gutters. November or April, the wasps would be gone or comatose, and I would just whack their little paper nests with my trowel and forget about them before they reached the ground. But this was July, and I was high above the gutters, clinging to the steep roof, struggling to reach the front dormer soffits with paint brush and bucket of primer.

It had started with the second floor sleeping porch in back, which my father believed to have been added in the thirties. He tediously pointed out the lousy job they had done—too little pitch on the shed roof to drain once the untrussed two by fours bowed, too little space between roof and ceiling to insulate or ventilate. Every winter, when we got a thaw after a week or two of sub-zero weather, the beaded board ceiling inside would weep all over with condensation melt. I tacked up heavy plastic sheets under the ceiling to funnel the rusty drainage into five gallon buckets, which I emptied into the toilet every morning. The damp wood buckled and mildewed, until finally last fall we hired a contractor to rebuild the sleeping porch with a proper gable roof and re-shingle the whole house.

He squandered November and a freakishly mild December and January, arriving finally in February with a demolition crew that knocked down the sleeping porch to knee walls and stubs of corner pillars, covered it all with a huge blue tarp, and disappeared. Sara and I would lie in bed listening to the fabric rustling and snapping in the wind all night like a ship under sail, and in the morning the bedroom was flooded with blue light.

On the first of March, a heavy, wet snowfall bowed the tarp down to the porch floor. Stray nails pierced the plastic, and water pooled and bled through the kitchen ceiling below as the snow melted. That got the contractor back. His carpenters framed and sheathed the new sleeping porch, and a crew of Mexican roofers arrived, ran their aluminum ladders up the sides of our house, and went to work with garden forks, ripping off layer after layer of shingles down to the old roof boards.

I tried to talk with them when they were up there, a casual ¡Hola!, a ¿Cómo están? They ignored me. The weather turned hideously cold, dry snow whipping across the underlayment, wind rattling their ladders, but they kept humping bundles of shingles up to the roof, banging them down. They found rotten wood on the overhangs, and the building inspector made us replace the soffits with new beaded fir because we're in the historic district. Dollar a board foot, eight hundred feet of it. Four months later, that new wood was what I was trying to paint, crawling up beneath the eaves, precariously working sideways, backwards, twisted around.

I had finished the soffits on the south side of the dormer, worked my way back to the roof edge, and climbed down a stepladder to the front porch roof when I saw Jerry Biggs crossing the street from the park, a guy who used to be our neighbor two doors away until his wife kicked him out. I turned to shift my stepladder to the north side of the dormer but wasn't quick enough. He waved and shrugged his ever-present green backpack so it hung from one shoulder. He had seen me see him. I waved back but kept going with the ladder, set it in place on the other side of the porch roof, crouched to change the c-clamped leveling board from the right leg to the left.

"Isaiah! Hey, man, need any help?"

I waited for his handsomely-freckled, light-skinned face to appear at the top of the extension ladder leading up to the porch roof. When it didn't, I straightened, walked over to the edge, and said hi to him, thanks, I was good. He was expecting me to climb down and exchange a black-power handshake with him, the way he had always greeted me.

"How you doing, Jerry?" I squatted at the edge of the porch roof, one hand resting on a rung of the ladder. Must have looked as if I were steadying it for him, or maybe getting ready to shove it over if he started to climb. I crossed my arms on my knees.

"Brother, I bear good tidings," he said. "They're bringing my show back. Completely new set and shit. Sunday morning, kinda early, but we're working on that. I got a meeting with them this afternoon, and I am *pumped*."

"That's terrific, Jerry," I said. He used to have a cable-access show focused on race relations, "Minnesota Ice," where he would interview minority leaders and get them going on the hypocrisy of social service agencies and the brutality of the police. The show was cancelled after he started drinking again, which was also the last straw for his wife. "Sounds like you're doing really well," I said.

"Doing *great*," he said. "Thanks, Isaiah. I appreciate your support, you've always been there for me, man."

I couldn't remember when I had ever been there for him, except maybe that I listened patiently when he would catch me outside and give me a blow-by-blow of a broadcast or complain about how the station executives were screwing him. He had talked about having me on the show, maybe on a panel of black educators, but nothing came of it. "It's great seeing you again," I said, and stood up to get back to work.

"Man, you're freaking me out," he said, backing off a few steps as if he thought I might fall on him. "Come on down here where it's safe."

"My brush is caking up," I said. "In this heat you have to keep going." I moved a little closer to the roof edge, resting one paint-stiff gloved hand on the top of the ladder.

He took another step back. "You seen Susan?"

I said I hadn't. She always parked on the street, and her car was gone. She had moved all of his recording equipment and stereo crap to their garage after he moved out, and I wondered if he had come to retrieve it or thought he could patch things up. He looked as if he had been living rough, his dreadlocks matted and lopsided, his army jacket too heavy for July.

"I need the car to get out to this meeting," he said. "Fucking Eden Prairie." He stared at the front porch of Susan's house but made no move to go ring the bell. He knew she wasn't home.

"I have to get back to work," I said, and retreated to the stepladder I was using to get from the porch roof up to the main roof of the house, above the third-floor attic. I thought about my Civic in the garage, the first new car I've ever owned. I couldn't see Jerry anymore from where I was, but I called down to him, "I'll tell Susan you stopped by, if you want me to."

After a minute I saw him heading back across the street into the park. I thought he maybe would wait on the bench near the sidewalk, but he disappeared into the trees, planning to catch the Selby bus back to Minneapolis, maybe, or maybe just walking. Since he had moved out, we would spot him every once in a while, trudging along in different neighborhoods. He never saw us, his eyes always fixed on the sidewalk ahead of him, his backpack looking stuffed with heavy objects.

I was trying to stop thinking about him as I edged up the main roof toward the hidden north eave of the dormer, dragging my bucket of primer on the wedge-shaped skid my father had rigged up out of scrap wood to hold the paint can upright on the sloping shingles. When I got around the corner of the dormer, something grazed past my ear and I jerked to the side, nearly losing my grip on the bucket. There was movement above my head—wasps, aliens darting and hovering around a nest the size of a volleyball, tucked up into the space where the dormer overhang meets the main roof. I flattened myself against the hot shingles and slid back down to the roof edge, feeling for the stepladder with my feet, fighting to keep the primer from spilling, hooking one foot into the top rung, wrestling myself onto the ladder, the skid falling, the bucket swinging and banging against the ladder, until I was able to regain the easier slope of the porch roof.

I retrieved the nearly-dry brush that had flown out of my hand, pressed the lid onto the paint can, and stood there, waiting for my heart to stop pounding. Before I climbed down the other ladder to the ground, I looked out over the park, trying to pierce the canopy of leaves. Jerry might still be there, a book open on his lap, watching from a park bench invisible to me from my second story perch. He always had books with him in that backpack, something that had at first made me think we would be friends, until I realized they were always the same books—*Soul on Ice, The Autobiography of Malcolm X*, and something about video production. He had long passages memorized, including from the video production book, and he liked to recite them in a dramatic way. He had a beautiful voice and a prodigious memory, but it always made me uncomfortable, standing there and listening to him.

I had to deal with the wasps, though, so I climbed down to the safe ground and went to the basement. Underneath my workbench I found an old can of wasp and hornet killer. It was rusty from the damp, but when I shook it and pointed it into the trash barrel and pressed the trigger, it sent a solid stream of insecticide shooting out. The heartless reek overflowed the barrel and filled the basement, and I retreated up the stairs, vaguely hoping the fumes would sicken the centipedes and silverfish that huddled behind the stucco somebody had used to coat the limestone walls and was now coming loose in big sheets. It irritated me when my father criticized the house and neighborhood, but he was right about one thing: people who owned the house before us had done some shoddy work.

The selling feature of this spray is that it kills on contact from twelve feet away. I climbed back up to the porch roof and read the instructions on the can. After warning not to spray indoors, it said, "Stand a safe distance from nest and not directly underneath. Point spray opening toward nest with wind at your back. Spray until nest is thoroughly wet. Hit wasps and hornets at rest where possible. Do not try to spray insects in flight."

Problem was, I found I couldn't see the nest while standing anywhere on the porch roof or even from the top of the stepladder leading up from the porch roof to the main house roof. It came into sight only as I crawled up onto the main roof and slithered myself around the side of the dormer. By then, I was only about five feet from the nest—not directly underneath it, but close enough to see the texture of its bulging paper walls, the entrance hole at the bottom, some cells they had framed in and not yet walled over. Lying on my side, I quietly shook the cool, rusty can, feeling the heavy poison swoosh around inside.

The best time for doing this job, according to the instructions, is early morning or evening. It was now about noon, but no wasps were visible at the moment, either flying or at rest. I squirmed around on the roof to get another foot or so of distance, the farthest away from the nest I could position myself and still have a clear shot. I raised the can, stretched out my arm, aimed at the tiny circular doorway. I pressed the trigger, and the poisonous stream drove itself like a spear into the heart of the nest. The nest seemed to explode, wasps hurtling out in all directions. I dropped the can and flung my arms up to protect my face, sending my glasses flying and losing my grip on the shingles. I slid backwards over the lip of the roof, missed the stepladder entirely, dropped eight feet to the porch roof, and sprawled there on my back, staring up into the sky's furious blur.

Eventually I was able to get back on my feet. I found my glasses, climbed down from the porch roof, and went inside. At the kitchen sink I scrubbed my hands with soap and steaming water until they no longer stank of insecticide.

I don't know if any of my wasps returned to the ruined nest and died from the residual action of the spray, as the can said they would, or whether they turned their backs forever on that catastrophe, flew out into the world singly or in little groups of refugees, seeking sanctuary under dry leaves or in old beer cans or stacks of firewood. None of them attacked me. If we meet again, I wonder if they might feel a connection, an awe or fear or hatred they can't explain.

The north soffit of the dormer is still not primed, much less painted. I keep waiting for my father to notice that I haven't finished the job, but from the ground you can barely see it, and he is getting stooped with age. From the ground you can't see the wasp nest at all. The wind might have knocked it down by now, blown it away like a crumpled fast food bag, or it might be hanging there still, a broken globe, waiting for my second coming.

WIDER, HIGHER, DEEPER

THE RIVER WAS wider than Franklin had expected, maybe a hundred, hundred and twenty feet across here, with standing waves like obsidian jammed against granite boulders, eddies where foam whirled obsessively and the fast water gnawed away beneath ledges of ice. It was early February. Franklin imagined himself wading the river when it was warmer, looping a fly line over trouty holes. He had recently developed a crush on Elena Rabe, whose cabin he and Alice were visiting for the first time, and watching this tough little river rush below it was like discovering another of her charms, unsuspected and full of promise. Elena and Alice were up in the cabin, fixing something for lunch. Franklin stared at the icy water and wished he had his fly rod with him right now. In his imagination, the birches that leaned pale trunks and dark, naked limbs over the water were clouded with shimmering green leaves. In his imagination, he was a hell of a fly fisherman.

A year ago, after his father died, Franklin Grosz had inherited a beautiful split bamboo Fenwick fly rod, never used, as far as anyone knew. His mother had found it with some of his father's old clothes in the basement. There was an expensive single-action reel, too, and a wet and a dry line, still in their wrappers. Tapered leaders. Tippet. Flies in an aluminum fly book. A set of neoprene hip boots.

Franklin didn't think his father even knew how to fly cast. When he was a boy, his father had taken him fishing sometimes, using spinning rods and reels, Zebcos from K Mart. They never caught much of anything, and as an adult Franklin had not pursued it. This past summer, however, he had taught himself to cast with the expensive, hand-crafted fly rod, sailing random flies out onto Lake Calhoun as joggers and rollerbladers dodged his back casts. Alice was a marathoner, and this gave him something to do while she trained. His consulting work for Deutsche Bank in Minneapolis left him with more free time than he needed, but so far he had never actually gone trout fishing.

Hands buried in his coat pockets, he shuffled his Sorels over the planks of the dock, pushing snow into the black water. He pictured himself in the hip boots, working these eddies and pools while Elena watched from the deck of the cabin, leaning her soft, perfect arms against the railing. Alice, too, was standing there, lean and bronzed. Good luck, he could hear her calling out to him.

Then it was April, almost May, and Franklin and Elena had been lovers for a season. It didn't seem to bother her that she was having sex with her friend's boyfriend, and Franklin had decided to trust her judgment on this, her moral code was good enough for him. They had made love for the first time the day after he and Alice visited her in her cabin, and Franklin had never shaken the magic of the place, the pull of the river. When the long winter finally broke, he told Alice he was thinking of doing some trout fishing. Elena gave him the key to the cabin and said she maybe would be able to get away from the travel agency, but maybe not. That was how it worked for them, they got together when things fell their way. It was perfect.

Franklin took off early on Saturday morning, even before Alice had left for her long run, and had breakfast at a café in Circle City, a regular old time place with weak, abundant coffee and cinnamon rolls the size of cabbages. He walked across the street to a tackle shop for a license and a trout stamp, though he doubted it was necessary this early in the year. "What're they taking out of the Little Straight these days?" he asked the man who was copying information from his driver's license.

"Smallmouth, mostly." The bass opener wasn't for another month or so, Franklin thought. The man said there were walleye, northern, largemouth.

"Trout?"

"They say there's nice trout in the Little Straight. Rainbow, brownies."

"What they catching them on?"

The man shrugged, not ambitious enough to make something up. He slid a set of regulations and a little waxed paper envelope for the license and trout stamp across the counter. Before he paid, Franklin wandered around the store, picking up some double-ought Mepps spinners, tapered leaders, tiny poppers, whatever looked good, and brought them to the counter. There was a sawed off, pump action, twelve gauge shotgun on display behind the clerk. With matt-black pistol grip and barrel like a piece of iron pipe, it looked out of place among the walnut-stocked deer rifles and engraved hunting shotguns and target pistols with fantastically sculptured handles. "That's some firearm," Franklin said as the clerk rang up his purchases.

He didn't have to turn around, he knew what Franklin was talking about. "Yeah," he said. "They call that the Camper's Special."

Franklin laughed. "Sell a lot of them?"

"There's a lot of campers around here. Want to take a look?" He lifted it down and handed it over the counter, and Franklin hefted it as if he knew what he was doing. The only way to fire it would be blasting away from the hip, an ugly business.

"Feels good, don't it?"

"Feels great." He handed it back and walked out of the store with gun oil haunting his nostrils.

It was not easy finding the cabin. Even this early in the year, trees and brush had leafed out enough to change the contours and texture of the woods, which he had seen only in winter. Several times he had to pull over and tramp a ways into the trees along the river where he thought Elena's cabin ought to be, before he came to her turnoff and the overgrown lane. He unlocked the padlocks securing a sheet of plywood over the door, but it seemed like too much effort to remove the window coverings. Enough light streamed in from the higher windows of the A-frame to give the cabin a church-like coziness.

Instead of getting a fire going in the wood stove, Franklin just kept his jacket on as he put his father's beautiful fly rod together on the kitchen table and made coffee and ate a roll he had brought from the restaurant. He needed the coffee. Though he had drunk three or four cups in town, he felt sluggish and lazy, and he put off all morning the business of pulling on the hip boots and plodding down to the river. He climbed the ladder to the loft bedroom and lay on the bare foam mattress, enjoying the view of lacy, pale green treetops, sunlight filtering down and glinting up from the otherwise-invisible river far below. When that grew old, he climbed down and dragged a chaise longue out onto the deck and lay in the sun reading some magazines he found in the cabin and listening for the roar of Elena's old bug-eyed Porsche pulling in behind his Audi.

Finally he hoisted himself out of the chaise and went for a walk, making a stop at the outhouse, then taking the stairs that zigzagged down to the river. The river was higher than it had been in Febru-ary, now almost licking the underside of the dock extending a few yards from the end of the stairs. From there, Franklin could look far downstream. He spotted, glimmering almost white in the distance, the towering dead pine tree that held in its topmost branches a mass of something that Elena had pointed out in February as an eagles' nest. While he watched, shading his eyes from below against the glare off the water, a speck rose from the tree and circled out of sight.

He climbed back up to the cabin and found the binoculars that Elena kept in a drawer there—foolishly, he thought, given the like-lihood of break-ins in a place left unoccupied so much of the year. Still, better to have a two hundred dollar pair of binoculars stolen than to frustrate thieves into trashing your place, he supposed. They were wonderful binoculars, huge, powerful things, 10 x 50, heavy and steady in his hands, colors crisp and undistorted to the very edges. He sat on the chaise, propped his elbows on his knees, and found the tree and the outsized nest.

While he watched, something landed on a branch a little to one side of the nest and perched there, so still he might have missed it if he hadn't seen it fly in and stretch its wings, shifting itself on the branch like a chicken before it settled down. Next to the bulk of the nest, it looked tiny, even through the binoculars, yet he could make out the white head, the dark body and wings. He watched until his eyes ached, waiting for something to happen. The eagle finally hopped toward the nest, wings half-spread for balance, flapped to the lip of the nest, then was gone, whether into the nest or flown away Franklin didn't know, though he thought he hadn't even blinked. He watched through the glasses and scanned the painfully blue sky above the river but caught no further sight of the eagle.

The sun was getting high, jabbing down through the thin canopy of leaves. Elena wasn't going to show up, he decided, as long as he was just hanging around on her deck. He would have to get into the river, he would have to have a line stretching out into the fast water, as he had imagined himself back in February. She would come out onto the deck and watch him for a while, admiring the graceful slow lift of the fly rod, the line looping and straightening behind him, whipping forward and settling onto the water. At last call down to him. That was how he pictured it, and he had learned to trust his visualizations.

He finished the coffee, visited the outhouse again, then unloaded the rest of his gear and two bottles of wine from the trunk of his car. He slipped on his fishing vest, most of its innumerable pockets still empty even after stashing the tackle he had bought that morning, pulled up the hip boots, tied their inner webbing above his knees, and buckled them to his belt. He picked up his father's Fenwick and clomped down to the river, threading the long, delicate antenna of split bamboo ahead of himself through the overhanging branches. At the bottom of the stairs, he picked his way to the water's edge and dipped his hand into its hard rush. In seconds the hand tingled and went numb, and he wondered whether there was enough insulation in the boots.

When he stepped into the water, he had to grab at the dock for support. The footing was treacherously slippery—rounded, mossy rocks on which the rubber soles of the boots slid as if they had been greased. You needed felt soles for this. The boots were the only thing in his father's mysterious stash of fly fishing gear not top of the line.

He moved gingerly out into the river, looking for stretches of gravel where the going would be easier, feeling the icy water rise past his knees, pressing the rubbery fabric of the boots tight around his legs.

Before he had left the cabin, Franklin had tied on one of the tiny Mepps spinners, and he now cast it ahead of him, short casts at first, wary of the tree branches reaching out from shore, then, with the stream itself behind him, full casts folding and unfolding themselves toward the eddies swirling flat beyond boulders and half-submerged logs. Pretty good casts, though he didn't really know what to do once the line lay in a long squiggle ahead of him except to twitch it a little, the way his father had shown him how to enliven a spinning lure, and then lift the line off the water with an upward sweep of the rod, let it straighten behind him, and whip forward again.

The stream was deeper than he had expected, and he was only able to wade about a third of the way across it before the dark water lapped up to the tops of his boots, a wave now and then slapping his crotch with shocking cold. He should have had chest-high waders, with felt-soled wading shoes. About two hundred yards of the river was visible from the deck of the cabin. He thrashed every part of it he could reach without hanging up his back casts or wading beyond the limits of his hip boots, casting downstream and across the current, working the spinner in past the rocks that would snag it from time to time, and an occasional submerged branch.

Usually he could tease the hook free when it snagged, moving upstream or down, edging as far out toward the obstruction as he dared, bending the long, supple rod in every direction to flip the lure away from the rocks between which it was jammed or tear it free from the sodden wood in which it was imbedded. By the time he could barely see the peak of the cabin's steep roof above the trees and must have been out of sight from its deck, he had lost two spinners, switched to a dry fly, lost it in a careless back cast, and tied on another Mepps, which he tried to keep a little off the bottom.

Franklin wasn't much of a fisherman, really, and every time he looked back and saw less of the cabin, or snagged his lure, or stepped into a hole deep enough to send a splash of icy water snaking down his hip boots, he considered turning back. But there was something seductive about it, something he had never felt while whipping a line out onto a city lake. You send out a part of yourself, thin as thought, to dart about blindly as tons of water surge around it. From your shoulder and arm and wrist and hand to the cork grip to the long weightless rod to the sweep of buoyant line to the nylon leader tapering almost to nothing to the thread of tippet to the tiny bristle of the lure and the minute flash of its spinner catching a fleck of light in the furious water to the hair-thin hook to the barb to the infinitely fine point it's one continuous thing, it's all of it you, including the river. Like sex, an intimate eyelash of violence, vulnerable and dangerous and unblinkingly ready. That was what he felt, moving slowly through the water, though he did not think a word of it. That was what kept him going forward, though his mind was back in the cabin, on the foam mattress, waiting for Elena.

He kept working down the river. Occasionally he would get a view of the eagles' nest ahead of him, sometimes catch a brief sweep of wings above the treetops. He stopped to rest on a gravel bar. He had been wading farther and farther downstream between casts, getting picky, stopping to cast only where the water roiled most sensually at the foot of a boulder or into the shadows beneath a tree leaning over the water. He spotted an eagle drifting overhead, then a second one in the sky at the same time, the mate.

He looked around. At some point he had passed into wilderness. There had been occasional cabins along the river for maybe a half-mile down from Elena's, none of them occupied, as far as he could tell. Here there was nothing but woods. On the meadow flats across the river from Elena's place, somebody had hauled in a trailer home and set up a picnic table and strung clothesline, but this year's spring floods had flung the table into a stand of aspen, and the trailer sat heeled over in the mud, probably beyond hope of rescue until the middle of summer.

They were rednecks, Elena had said in February, as he and Alice had looked across the river from her deck. Always chainsawing trees and playing music as loud as their big tape decks could produce and screwing with the shoreline, hauling out rocks and leaving styrofoam and beer cans.

"How do they get down there?" Franklin had asked her. "No roads, are there?"

She didn't know how they had gotten the trailer in. They drove a four-wheel-drive something, big Jeep thing. And the kids tore around on one of those off-road three wheelers and a trail bike. "They disappear in the winter," Elena said. He had wrapped his arm around Alice's shoulders for warmth, her thin arms firm beneath the down jacket, and met Elena's dark, happy eyes. The three of them had listened from the snowy deck, wine glasses cradled in gloved hands, and heard nothing but wind rattling in the bare trees and hissing in the pines.

Franklin had heard no human sound from the river today. He was tired and cold and hungry and needed to get back to the cabin. He could no longer visualize catching anything, and by now Elena might have arrived. The bed made up. The woodstove crackling. Besides, he was down to his last lure, a hopelessly unattractive purple bug. He stood up on the gravel bar and waded into the river one more time, and began wondering whether there might be an easier way to get back to the cabin than retracing his steps through the river, swinging his legs against the stubborn, relentless push of the current. Except for the occasional gravel bars, which were often separated from each other by treacherously deep, fast channels, the slippery cannonball bottom at Elena's dock had continued all the way down the river.

As he waded toward the center of the river and paid out line for his last series of casts, the eagles' nest came into view again, its bulk overwhelming now, the great tree beneath it towering over the river. For some time it had been what was drawing him forward, though he hadn't thought about it. If the river continued to be wadeable, or if the shore were passable, perhaps he could get right under it. He reeled in the line until the tapered leader was inside the guides and the hook of the bug snagged on the tip top eyelet.

Concentrating only on wading forward, he made better time. As he came in sight of the eagles' nest again, maybe another three-quarters of a mile away, both shores had flattened out and the river had broken itself among gravel bars and sand bars, snaky islands where he could rest from the slog and push of water. Farther down, on his right, the opposite bank started to rise. Franklin saw that the great tree supporting the nest stood far up on an eroding cliff that turned the river to the left. He wouldn't be able to get to the tree itself, not in the clumsy hip boots, but now he could see the eagles, both of them, circling the tree, sailing out of sight, returning.

He leaned back against a boulder jutting from the shore and watched them. He was tired of balancing on slippery rocks. He had come far enough, it was enough just to sit there and watch the eagles come and go, enjoy the solitude, the budding woods. It was enough, he thought, even by itself. Even without Elena. He imagined her in the cabin, kneeling in front of the woodstove.

He studied the landscape. While the right bank climbed higher and higher from the river's elbow, the bank to his left spread out into a hummocky meadow, with stands of wispy tamarack as open and sunny as a park. Wading the river had been hard work, and most of the way trees and brush had overhung the water's edge. The stretch of shore ahead of him to the left, by contrast, was open and inviting. Without much investment of time or effort he could walk along the shore to a point opposite the eagles' nest, as close to them as he could hope to get, and then maybe he would be able to find a trail up to the road that must run parallel to the river. He remembered driving in through an area of scrub and open ground like this. He could find it. He imagined himself strolling along the smooth gravel shoulder. The distant growl of Elena's approaching Porsche.

The bank was low but muddy. When he was clambering up the short, steep slope, his foot slid out from under him, and in his struggle to catch himself he came down on the grip section of the rod with a sickening dry cracking sound. The extravagantly expensive rod had come with a spare tip, but nobody was expected to break the butt end, you would have to be an idiot. Cursing, Franklin dragged himself up onto the thick tufty grass, then looked for the damage. He couldn't see any. Tenderly, then with more force, he put stress on the section without finding even a weakened spot. He went up the rod foot by thinning foot. It was a miracle. A dead stick on the ground must have made the horrible sound, but still it seemed like a miracle, and he would not have been more pleased and surprised if he had thrown a ruined rod into the river and a woman's arm had risen out of the water with a new one in her hand.

He thought about his father as he carefully broke the rod down, ferrule by ferrule, used a length of leader to tie the sections together in a neat bundle, and hiked on along the river bank. He felt as if he had made a point, proven something to his father, who had never trusted his judgment, who had always expected the worst.

The ground was marshy, and he had to jump at times from one grassy hump of earth to another, an awkward business in the clumsy hip boots. On the other hand, in hip boots it didn't matter if he slipped once in a while and went into the mucky water up to his knees. He had never played football, but he imagined it must be a terrific feeling, clacking around in helmet and shoulder pads (and hip pads and elbow pads and knee pads and groin cup and God knows what else), so thoroughly protected. Even knowing that you were going to be hurt anyway, that you were going to feel pain, it must be sweet to wear armor against the most serious threats.

He felt armored in his father's great, high boots, magically protected. The insulation he had been worried about had, in fact, kept his feet perfectly comfortable in the icy water. He strode across the marsh. Just as he entered the tamarack grove, a massive shadow swept across him, he ducked, and a voice of extraordinary, piercing ugliness screamed at him. Screamed, anyway. But it must have seen him. The tamaracks were so lightly needled they looked dead and provided only a scrim of cover.

He walked as carefully as he could to the edge of the thin wood, making no sounds except the suck of mud beneath his boots. Even before the stand of trees gave out and bog took over again, the ground seemed to be getting softer. Above the high sandy bank and the towering pine with that truckload of tangled branches secured somehow in its dead crown, one of the eagles banked and screamed and flew off and almost immediately returned, or its mate did, he couldn't tell them apart. The terrible energy of their wheeling flight seemed unnatural. They seemed too big for the air to bear them, as even the enormous tree seemed too slight to sustain their huge nest.

Franklin's presence obviously bothered the eagles. He knew that people now and then floated in rubber boats down the Little Straight during the summer, but a man on foot must have been unusual here. Across the open stretch of marsh ahead of him, the land started to rise again. That was where he imagined that he could pick up the road. From up there he would also have a better view of the nest. He might be able to see if there were hatchlings yet, a possibility that thrilled him, information that would be delicious to share.

He was reluctant at first to come out into the open again, however. It wasn't hard to imagine the eagles attacking someone lurking so close to their nest. He knew they wouldn't, but it wasn't hard to imagine it. He hesitated a few minutes before strolling out as casually as he could, veering a ways off of a direct course to the higher ground in order to appear as unmenacing as possible.

A line of dense brush kept him from making as wide a circle as he had planned. When he came to a backwater stream cutting its way through the quivery green hummocks, running without a sign of motion in its dark water except the almost imperceptibly slow drift of a leaf toward the river, he had to abandon discretion for the time being and scout up and down before choosing the best place to cross. The first two places he tried proved deeper than they looked, the squishy bottom sucking him almost to the middle of his thighs before he managed to drag himself back. He crouched as an eagle passed overhead so close that he could see the spread, individual feathers of its wingtips and the scales of its legs. The bundled fly rod wasn't much of a weapon, but he gripped it like a club.

He got to the other side of the backwater finally by hanging onto a branch he had dragged over and laid across the stream, pulling himself hand over hand, churning through the deep mud and turning the still water cloudy black, until he could stumble up again onto the lush, tall grass. He rested for a while on the cushiony ground, looking up into the empty sky. The eagles were either in the outrageous nest or had flown off somewhere. His thrashing in the stream might have scared them off.

He rested on his elbows on the damp, spongy vegetation and considered which path to follow to the rising ground. The marsh was expressionless, indistinguishable rolling green islands in a mostly invisible sea of muck, an occasional scrub tree or jagged, dead stump thrusting upward. He set off again. Within a few yards he was crossing a swath of tar-black mud, and in two steps he found myself up to his knees in muck again.

This time he had more trouble pulling his feet free from the ooze. He felt himself sinking with the struggle and pushed down on the muck surrounding him, using the bundled rod for purchase. He tried to walk his sluggish legs forward in the muck, bicycled in slow motion, found no bottom.

He forced himself to stop struggling, let himself settle into a point of equilibrium. Once he got himself free, he decided, he would walk back to the river and take his chances with the slippery but solid rocks and icy water that would push against him in honest, straightforward opposition. He pictured it, the effort, the relief at the end. He caught his breath, waited for his heart to stop pounding. He started again, with more careful, cunning movements.

But he couldn't get anywhere, sank farther, and in a few minutes the stinking muck coldly enveloped his crotch and welled over into his boots. It slithered down into the loose tops of the boots and became the boots, settling around his legs and hauling him down.

He had to get out of the boots. Even while holding still, he thought he could feel himself sinking further. The boots were heavy as lead. He managed to unbuckle the belt straps after an eternity of fumbling in the slime that covered them. Sweating with the effort, he removed his fishing vest and laid it and the bundled rod ahead of him, where there was a mat of mossy green beyond the mud. He shoved one hand through the muck inside a boot, struggling to reach and release the inner lacing that held it snug above the calf. He couldn't do it, the pressure of the mud prevented him from reaching even to the knee. He couldn't get enough grip to roll the boot top down, and although he thought he finally managed to touch the top of the canvas webbing, the laces were out of reach. Even if he could have thrust his hand down far enough, he doubted that he could have gotten the heavy snaps undone.

He realized with a jolt that the struggle was tipping him off balance, toppling him, and he flailed to stay upright. He gave up on the boots and forced himself to be still for a while, to think and not move. The ooze had reached the top of his belt, his torso and arms were sludged with it, his face splattered, the grit and taste of it in his mouth. He listened to a red wing blackbird whistling somewhere. Far off, one of the eagles screamed. The wind rattled last year's dead cattails. He squirmed, had to piss. He pissed, the heat spreading around his groin. He shivered and struggled into the fishing vest again.

There were still several hours of daylight, but it was starting to get cold, the sky beginning to cloud over. If it rained, he would be in trouble. He could die of hypothermia. He didn't think he would drown, he wasn't willing to imagine that happening, the rotting ooze sliding into his nostrils, between his lips, filling his ears and the sockets of his eyes.

At least he wasn't sinking any more, or not very fast, as long as he was quiet. He just hung there, suspended with the surface a few inches above his waist, held in the terrible softness. He shouted, didn't even hear an echo. He had been shouting for help off and on ever since he realized he was stuck, though he was certain no one could hear him. There was no reason for anyone to be within earshot. One of the eagles returned and swooped in low—curious, perhaps, at his loss of stature, or emboldened by his motionlessness. Eagles ate carrion, he remembered. He waited for it to soar over again, and thought with longing of the Camper's Special.

He looked around at the hummocky meadow. About thirty feet behind him, there was a scrubby tree of some kind, maybe chokecherry, he thought for some reason, though he didn't really know what a chokecherry tree looked like. Nothing closer. He probed and prodded with the bundled rod. Everywhere he pressed, the rod sank into mud. Even where there was lush green turf, it floated on ooze. Bubbles rose to the surface, bulged, burst pungently.

The foot of the bluff was maybe a hundred yards ahead of him. He imagined himself resting on the top of it, looking over at the eagles' nest. From up there he probably could hear the hum of an occasional car or truck on the county road. If Elena drove by, he would hear the rowdy Porsche and follow it to the cabin. An eagle crossed the sky. He followed it out of sight.

Moving as little as possible (any movement still seemed to settle him deeper in the stinking mud, he couldn't keep his elbows out of it anymore), he untied the mucky bundle of fly rod sections. He fitted the rod together, sucking muck out of the finely machined ferrules, spitting it out. He clipped off the tapered leader about a yard from the line, worked the thick, stiff nylon through the eyelet of the ugly bug, and tied a hard, fat knot. With his clipper, he trimmed all the bristle from the lure, then stripped off some line. He managed to twist himself around, till he almost faced the scrubby tree. Casting awkwardly, he made several cautious false casts, paying out gradually, then drove the line as hard as he could toward the tree's branches. It fell to the ground, yards short of the tree. He collected the line and tried again, paying line out on both back and forward casts. It didn't seem so far to the little tree, but he couldn't reach it. Finally he noticed that he had somehow whipped off the lure, the leader ended in nothing but a little crimp. Even if he reached the tree, he couldn't snag anything.

He laid the rod aside, butt end and reel resting on a hummock of grass, the double taper line still meandering gracefully toward the chokecherry or whatever it was. His father's retirement rod. A treat for himself, a luxury he had never used.

The sun was getting low. The eagles had stopped their swooping surveys and apparently had roosted, though there was at least an hour of light left. He no longer made them nervous. They would check him out in the morning. He discovered how much he hated them. If he had that Camper's Special, he would have fired shot after shot into their brutal truckload of sticks. He wanted buckshot, he wanted slugs. He clutched a fistful of the mud that surrounded him and hurled it. It didn't even reach the river between him and the bluff on which the eagles' nest stood. It was too soft, it wouldn't hold together.

After a while, the tantrum passed and Franklin wiped his mucky hands on the long, coarse grass. He was so tired. Somebody would come looking for him and haul him out eventually. There was no other place he could be, a trout fisherman. He was cold and drowsy, he needed to rest. He wondered dully if Elena had decided to come up to the cabin, after all. She might be looking down the river, looking through the binoculars he had left on the kitchen table. Even this late, she could see the eagles' nest. She couldn't see him. The eagles could see him.

He was so tired. He tried to imagine rescue, but he couldn't, he was too tired. He closed his eyes, then opened them again, thinking he felt something sweep overhead. Gazing up at the untroubled gray expanse, he let himself lean backwards, let his arms settle onto the accommodating muck. He spread his arms over the still surface of the swamp, staring up at the empty sky.

His face was stiff with drying muck. He had a hard time keeping his eyes open. His tired arms, and then his lower back settled into the muck as he leaned backwards, and the muck crept across his stomach. He was so tired, he closed his eyes and leaned back, let himself tip back farther and farther in the muck, as if falling backward in slow motion, falling backward so slowly, it was not even unpleasant.

Something stirred, though he was too tired to notice it. The stirring was too slight, too distant to register on his almost sleeping mind. Still, deep in the blackness around him, beneath him, something stirred. As if he were falling, his shoulders and then the back of his head eased farther back into the pillowy muck, as if he were falling, slowly, slowly backward.

But he was not falling. He was floating. His almost forgotten legs in his father's cheap waders were floating slowly upward. Slowly, effortlessly, he was floating upward.

FORTUNATELY

WALT WAS OF an age when a man spends a lot of time standing before urinals and toilets, meditating on this or that until his prostate,
that powerful argument against Intelligent Design, decides he has
waited long enough. Fortunately, there was a window at eye level
in the bathroom, overlooking his back yard, where a squirrel was
running along the back fence toward the garage. It leaped up and
a little backward off the gatepost to catch the overhanging garage
roof, a maneuver Walt knew must happen regularly, judging from
the claw-shredded post cap, but he had never seen it before. It raced
along the roof ridge, jumped down onto the side fence, and disappeared up into the branches of a maple tree that had been struggling
all its life under the vast, sloppy canopy of a cottonwood tree, a hundred and ten feet tall, its deeply fissured trunk twenty feet around,
one of the biggest trees in Saint Paul. This spring, as it struggled to
leaf out, the aged cottonwood had dropped eight garbage barrels of
twigs into Walt's yard alone. He couldn't calculate how many must
have dropped into the neighbors' yard, where the huge, grotesque
tree erupted out of an otherwise perfect lawn.

Before zipping up, he saw his neighbor Corvin, barefoot and
wearing sweat pants and an undershirt, step out onto his deck with
what Walt guessed was an air rifle. He aimed up into the maple tree's
crown, held it for an irritatingly long time, then fired with a little
cracking sound. Instantly something dropped and crashed into the
ferns on Walt's side of the fence. Walt waited for Corvin to come
around the fence to retrieve it, but instead he pumped the lever of
the air rifle a few times, then stalked around the yard for a while,
aiming now and then into the branches of the maple tree, but not

firing again. Finally he went back into the house.

Walt stood at the bathroom window, waiting for him to come for the squirrel he had shot. He didn't come, and eventually Walt saw him leave the house in coat and tie and drive away. His aim fixed among the tree branches, he must not have seen the squirrel fall, must have blinked, must have thought he had missed.

Walt went outside to his back yard and found the squirrel lying in some crushed ferns next to the fence. He poked it with a stick to confirm that it was dead. He couldn't see a wound, but when he flipped it over with the stick, there was a small bloody hole right behind its ear, a perfect shot. Walt didn't think he should have to dispose of the murdered animal. He thought of calling Corvin or leaving him a note, but it was awkward that he had watched and not said anything before Corvin left, and if he hadn't seen the shooting, how would he know who was responsible? Finally Walt got his trash grabber from the garage, clamped it around the squirrel's still-limp body, and flung it over the fence.

Walt intended to talk with Corvin about the matter, but he still hadn't said anything two weeks later, when a crew came with dump trucks and a huge hydraulic claw and a 180 foot crane on a flatbed semi-trailer and a wood chipper big enough to swallow a queen size bed to cut down the enormous cottonwood, which had taken forever to leaf out that summer after the weeks of branch dropping and had been judged by a consulting arborist to be reaching the end of its more or less 125 year life span. The monstrous crane reached from the street where it was parked, over Walt's back yard, to the middle of Corvin's yard, where the great, doomed tree towered. Neighbors set up lawn chairs behind Corvin's yard to watch the operation, many of them with cameras, and even the tree-cutting crew stopped work now and then to take pictures with their cell phones.

Walt sat next to Corvin as the enormous crane swung cut sections of the tree over his house, branches that looked big enough crossing the sky, but when they were lowered to the street to be further dismantled, stood taller than his third story attic window, each section a big, full grown tree in itself. He thought of telling Corvin that he had seen him shoot that squirrel, but found himself caught between shame at having tossed the body over the fence and resentment that Corvin had not taken care of it himself.

Corvin aimed his video camera upward as another tree-sized branch of the cottonwood made its way across the sky, and said, "You don't see that every day."

CRAWL SPACE

ELDER CROWN PULLED on his overcoat and sat down again at the kitchen table across from his son, Isaiah, who lowered the newspaper he had been reading and said, "You want to switch places? That window must still leak." Isaiah had covered it with clear plastic that is supposed to shrink smooth, but there were ripples stretching out like fingers where he hadn't been patient enough to do a neat job.

"It isn't the window. It's the floor. Coming in through the foundation. Window's fine." The window wasn't fine, but it was the icy air snaking up his leg from underneath that was offending him.

"We're over the crawl space here. I insulated it last summer."

"Old house like this got a hundred secret places weather comes in." He didn't say what automatically came to mind: old ghetto house like this.

"You have to have some ventilation."

"Ventilation. This isn't ventilation. This is frostbite." Elder slid his chair back and started tucking his wool trouser legs into his socks.

"For God's sake, Dad, switch places." His son crumpled the newspaper onto the table, scraped his chair back, rose.

Elder stayed put, finishing with his socks, and after a minute his son sat down. "Must've built this addition in the thirties," the old man said. "Dust bowl years—'36, '37. Hot as hell." He leaned back and ran a skinny hand over the alligatored varnish of a pantry bin. "Your Aunt Sophie came up to Minnesota in the summers with a white family she worked for then, and she said everybody building sleeping porches. So hot, people slept in the parks some nights. Somebody built that sleeping porch upstairs and slapped this room under it over just a crawl space, never thinking about the winter. Never thinking about

145

nothing except how damn hot they were."

"More coffee?" Sara, his daughter-in-law, refilled his cup. "Why don't you come with us?" she said. "I feel bad, leaving you here alone."

He was in exile from his own home, which was being shown to prospective buyers, the second tedious weekend of open houses. A house he had built fifty years before in a new suburb of Minneapolis, where he had raised his family and had always expected to die, though in that his wife had stepped impatiently ahead of him. For a year and a half, now, he had been alone, and when Sara and his son had broached the subject of his selling and moving in with them, he had surprised himself as much as them by agreeing it was time to move. Not to live with them in inner city St. Paul, however. He signed a rental agreement at a senior high-rise a mile or so from his house in Richfield, a first-ring Minneapolis suburb, but he wouldn't be moving in for another month. "I'll be glad for a little peace and quiet," he said.

The family was walking over to his grandson's school a block away to work a fundraising carnival. A magnet school, they called it, trying to attract kids from nicer neighborhoods. Sara had baked trays of lemon bars, and Isaiah and Ike were going to run some game of skill or chance. "Don't worry about me," he said. Ike came in from watching cartoons and poured himself a mountainous bowl of cereal, then added milk in a wavering stream, drops splattering from the dry flakes onto the table.

Elder reached over with a paper napkin and wiped up the boy's mess. "When I went to build my house, I built for the Minnesota winter. Full basement. We never had no drafts. You remember a draft all the time you were living at home?"

"No sir, you built a solid house."

"Better believe I did. I told that realtor, 'Now's the time to sell this house, coldest time of the year. You sell it to somebody appreciates a tight house.'"

"It's tight now, all those new windows and doors. Good thing they gave you a new furnace, too. You'd be suffocating yourself with that old octopus."

"Nothing wrong with that furnace." Elder's house, near the Twin Cities airport, had been included in a noise-abatement program, and last spring they had replaced every window and exterior door, added insulation, replaced his ancient furnace with a tiny gas burner, and installed a whole-house air conditioner so he could stay inside with the windows closed year round and not hear the jet airplanes.

All of it free. He just had to move his stuff away from the windows. A crew arrived and pulled out every frame and casing and sash down to the rough openings, put in new insulated glass windows with permanent screens and storms on tracks, heaved all the old wood and glass and screens and doors into a dumpster with the butchered carcass of his furnace, and hauled it away.

He had paid cash money for that furnace, and years later he had converted it to oil when he couldn't get coal delivered anymore. He had installed those old double-hungs with his own hands and had been wrestling with those wooden storms for fifty years. He had marked them and their corresponding sills in Roman numerals with a chisel, scraped and repainted them every five years, reputtied them he didn't know how often, swapped them with the screens every spring and swapped them back every fall.

Now you just slid the aluminum storm windows up and down on tracks. In deference to his age, they had rigged wires between the spring-loaded locking pins, so you could raise and lower them even with your hands crippled up with arthritis. Your hands could be useless as clubs and you could still do it, the foreman said.

There was nothing wrong with his hands. But he had let them go ahead and rig the wires on all the storm windows. When it got hot that summer, he turned on the air conditioner once to make sure it worked, and then turned it off again and opened his windows at night and closed them during the day and ran a fan, as he had always done.

He could live with a little heat. Freezing draft was another thing. When Isaiah and Sara and Ike were gone, he got down on his knees and ran a hand along the baseboard of the kitchen extension's outside walls. Then he went down to the basement and studied the situation. Separating the basement proper from the crawl space underneath the addition was the original foundation wall of rough limestone, pierced here and there with holes broken through for pipes, and a single leftover basement window, covered by a screen, that provided the only access to the crawl space. Beneath this window, Isaiah had set up a workbench, littered with jars of screws and nails, old paint cans, brushes that had been left soaking in turpentine so long they were rimed with congealed paint, and tools and leftover materials from a dozen household projects. Isaiah had been a willing helper when he was a boy, but he had never understood that a job was not finished until the mess was cleaned up and the tools put away.

Elder took off his overcoat, suit jacket, and tie, rolled up his sleeves, put on a denim shop apron, and started organizing things. He added turpentine to replace what had evaporated from around the brushes and worked the paint scum from the bristles with his fingers and rinsed them in the old wash tub with detergent and hot water. He arranged the jars on a shelf, sorted the tools into drawers, and used a brush to sweep off the workbench.

Then he hunted up a step stool and a trouble light on a long orange cord. With the help of the stool, he got himself up onto the workbench. He took a screwdriver to pry open the window screen, but didn't need it, for the screen hung loose in the frame, hinged at the top. He stuck his head and shoulders under the screen and shone the trouble light into the crawl space.

The long rear wall of the crawl space opposite him and the end wall a few feet to his left reflected whitely back, where Isaiah had insulated the foundation with styrofoam board. Leftover sheets of insulation were shoved to the side, and other things, hard to identify, lay around the window opening. A heavy, musty smell rose from the dirt floor.

Aiming the light in the other direction, peering down the length of the crawl space, he was able to see the far wall, the part of the crawl space underneath the kitchen. This wall, too, was covered with white styrofoam, but there was something odd about it. Where he was standing, sticking his head into the crawl space, there was no draft, nothing but the damp, still mustiness. But that far end was exactly where Isaiah would have gotten careless. Elder could imagine the cold air pushing in there. He stood on tiptoe, leaning in, stretching for it.

With some difficulty, he extracted his head and shoulders from the opening and its hanging screen, crawled down off the workbench, and climbed the two flights of stairs to Isaiah and Sara's bedroom. There he stripped to his long underwear and put on an old pair of overalls and a U of M sweatshirt he found in his son's closet. He folded his shirt and draped it beside his wool trousers over the footboard of the queen-size bed.

It was beyond his understanding why a man and woman who loved each other needed that much space. He and Marie, they had slept in a bed barely half this wide and never felt crowded. He sat for a few minutes on the edge of the bed, polishing his glasses with a cotton handkerchief he retrieved from the rear pocket of his suit trousers, before gathering himself and returning to the basement.

A set of crude wooden shelves Isaiah had built at the back of the workbench served as a ladder up into the crawl space. He propped open the screen with a broom handle, pushed the trouble light on its long cord in front of him, and eased himself stiffly through the little window. When his feet were through, he rolled onto his side and rested, propped up on one elbow, trying to catch his breath. After a while he started exploring with his free hand the junk that had been shoved in through the window—some flattened cardboard, a plastic dump truck, the leftover styrofoam boards. The earthen floor of the crawl space was cool and slightly damp. Isaiah should have covered it with plastic sheeting, the basement would be less musty.

When he had recovered, he got up on his hands and knees. Grabbing the handle of the trouble light and pulling as much cord through the opening as he dared without unplugging it, he crawled toward the far end. Cobwebs and miscellaneous wires draped along the underside of the joists brushed against the back of his head and neck. The dust and mold made him start to sneeze, until his nose ran and he could barely see for the tears. He cleared his nostrils one at a time, carefully snorting soot-clotted snot onto the earthen floor, then pulled out the big handkerchief and fashioned a mask, knotting it so that it cupped over his nose and beneath his chin.

Knees aching and the stringy muscles of his thighs and arms humming and burning with the strain, he reached the far end of the crawl space. He used the screwdriver to pry loose a piece of insulation from the end wall and it fell away, revealing not the concrete block that they had used in building the foundation for the addition in the thirties, but an older limestone wall, freezing cold beneath his hand. He studied it, then shone the light back along the length of the crawl space.

A tremor of excitement stirred in his veins. He was good at estimating distances, and he believed this end wall came too soon—there had to be another, blind space beyond it, maybe six or eight feet wide, before reaching the concrete block foundation wall. That was the part that was leaking cold air up into the kitchen. If he could get into that space, he could fix the problem.

The window over the workbench was a long, miserable crawl back, and he put it off for a while. He sat there in the glow of the trouble light, gathering his strength and longing for a cigarette. He had quit four years earlier, abruptly and without relapse, when Marie's emphysema had been diagnosed, and he couldn't smoke in this confined space anyway, but he would have liked to. It would have given him strength.

Finally he started the journey back to the window, leaving the trouble light where it was. By the time he stiffly wriggled, legs first, down onto the workbench again, his shoulders and hip joints and wrists and ankles and for some reason the arches of his feet ached, and his upper plate felt loose and foreign in his mouth from the strain of holding his head at such an awkward angle and grimacing behind the breath-damp mask. His heart thumped against his ribs, and there was a strange taste in his mouth, a stale pungency that made him think of old, crumpled money. He pulled down the mask and spat again and again into the trash barrel next to the workbench.

He was exhausted, his body achy as if from flu. He knew he should just pass his discovery on to Isaiah, let him deal with it. But the boy was prideful and skeptical of any advice he gave him. He had once looked at a spotless Oldsmobile that a member of Elder's church was practically giving away and called it a dinosaur. He would need proof.

After resting for a while, Elder assembled a few more tools of exploration—crowbar, electric drill, quarter-inch masonry bit—and climbed up onto the workbench. He shoved the tools ahead of him into the crawl space and wriggled up through the little window again. Crawling forward with the drill clomping in one hand and the crowbar in the other, he worked his way to the far end. Here he pulled off a second sheet of styrofoam, exposing the rest of a rough limestone wall. It must have been left over from the original structure, part of an entry stoop, probably, covered over when they extended the kitchen beneath the sleeping porch addition.

Behind that section of old foundation wall would be the uninsulated space directly underneath the kitchen table, full of writhing, icy winds. It was typical of Isaiah that he had just worked around the blind area, ignoring it, leaving the room above it unprotected. He and Sara had bought this old house in the inner city against Elder's advice, intending to fix its many problems. What they had actually done had been mostly cosmetic, or half-assed as this insulation job or the plastic-covered windows. A wound had to be wide open and bleeding before Isaiah would admit there was a problem.

Elder plugged the drill into a socket on the trouble light and pressed the bit into a mortar joint. The bit plunged in, the ancient mortar crumbling as he moved the drill from side to side, spraying sand and dust. Congratulating himself on the protection of his glasses and the improvised dust mask, he took the crowbar and jabbed at the mortar until one of the blocks sagged a little from the overhead floor joist. He pried it out farther and farther, walking it towards himself, until it tumbled to the floor with a muffled thud. He kneaded his thigh where the falling block had grazed it, then pulled the trouble light as far as its cord would allow, thrusting it into the opening. Across the chamber, maybe six feet away, he could make out the concrete block of the addition's exterior foundation wall. A dull cold pushed at him.

Trembling, he sat back in the cramped, chilly gloom, breathing through the damp mask, mechanically longing for a cigarette, rubbing his bruised leg. As he waited for his heart's thumping to ease, he thought about the space beyond the old limestone wall, which had been sealed off from the world sixty years before. He had been a young man then, in St. Louis, pushing wheelbarrows for a contractor during the day, reading the Bible at night. He had met Marie at Bible study. They had gotten married in that hot, hard time, 1937.

Marie had a miscarriage the next year, then another. After the war, Elder and his brothers had moved their families north to Minneapolis, settled in a new suburb too distracted by its own growth to notice them at first, a few black families building houses scattered among the other one-story houses and broad, bare yards, then willing to tolerate them. He and his brothers had started a commercial cleaning business, prospering as companies sprang up along the new interstate bypass.

Isaiah was born, their only child, and Marie had worried that he was alone too much, isolated in the white suburb. He would be happier in the city, she thought, or even moving back to St. Louis. But from the beginning Elder had seen where the future lay, and he had staked his claim to it, and held on. He had built a home with his own hands in the new housing development, and held on, and lived to see television broadcasts of race riots tearing through urban neighborhoods he might have settled for.

This neighborhood, for instance, a few blocks from the worst of those riots. This leaky old house Isaiah had chosen, a rebuke to Elder's calculation, though he had never said so. A different mix to raise his kids in, is what he had said, as if Richfield with them in it wasn't mixed. Reclaiming the inner city, he said, as if a sane man would want it.

No one ever burned down the suburbs. "Marie," Elder said. He had sworn to her that he would never raise his family in the ghetto. What more could a man do than find a safe place for his family? A new place, where they could prosper. Every American city at its heart was rotten with history. Isaiah thought he could change that, change history.

Shifting his position, Elder used the crowbar to pry loose a second block, this time working it inwards till it dropped ponderously on the far side of the wall, then pried beneath another block and eased it inch by inch from underneath the overlapping course, until he could topple it out of the way. Without stopping to rest, he levered four more stones free. As the last of them toppled into the hidden space, he felt the crowbar twist and drag out of his suddenly stupefied hands, drop, ringing against stone before sinking into the earthen floor, and his body followed it, falling forward into the opening, face down among the stone blocks and mortar dust, plunged suddenly into darkness.

He lay sprawled there, breathless, blind. After a while he dragged himself off the brutal stones onto the soft earth floor, rolled onto his back, and stared around through the glasses he could feel twisted on his face. He could see nothing, except somewhere in the distance a short, white thread that seemed to float in the darkness. He listened to his heart banging within his chest.

He struggled to get himself up into a sitting position, one hand raised to ward off the rough floor joists pushing down on him. He pulled the damp mask down from his face and ran a hand over his close-cropped skull. His hair and skin were stiff with dust. Feeling around, he found the trouble light, its aluminum shell and steel cage still warm. He must have yanked the long cord out of the wall socket when he fell. Folded between a low, invisible ceiling of wood and an invisible floor of earth, surrounded by stone, he closed his useless eyes. "Marie," he said, without noticing his own voice. "Marie," an emptiness. Not asking for anything, just pressing himself into a long-familiar hollow.

He opened his eyes to the darkness, the thread of light floating just out of reach, illuminating nothing. The sweatshirt was damp with sweat. He was cold. He fumbled for the trouble light to warm his hands with whatever heat was left in it, and it flickered on, then off again. He unsnapped the cage, twisted the warm bulb, and the low, cramped chamber materialized once more around him. The earthen floor was littered with rubble from the original construction, a hundred years before, or from when they had torn off the stoop and built the kitchen addition over it in the thirties, and this dirt had seen another moment of sun. A broken hammer handle. A crumpled, brittle newspaper. The stones he had levered free.

It was time for the long crawl out. But he remembered that thread of light, now invisible against the dimly illuminated foundation wall. He crawled toward where he thought it had been. An icy stream of air guided him as he approached it, until he could put his hand on the wall and found the blade of bitter cold cutting through a crack. "I know you," he said. It was the very shape of wind he had felt slicing up his trouser leg at breakfast. He unknotted the handkerchief from around his neck and used the screwdriver from his pocket to stuff the damp cloth into the crack.

The silence was deeper now. He listened to his heart thudding, the rasp of his breath. Then, something else. He froze there on his hands and knees, straining to hear over the roaring of his own blood. He crawled back to the opening he had made in the old limestone foundation wall. In the darkness that hung in the crawl space beyond, he sensed it again. He braced himself against the rough limestone and listened. He couldn't move, couldn't call out, only managed to shape his lips around an emptiness. He held himself so still, he felt himself disappearing into the stone, the earth. An emptiness, come for him. Marie. Marie.

And then it was gone. His hand found the trouble light, burning like a pale fire beside him. Kneeling under the floor joists, his heart banging inside his chest like a machine shaking loose from its mountings, he raised the light and let it reach through the stone gap into the long crawl space darkness.

"You, boy," he said.

"Grandpa."

It was Ike, crouched at the far end of the crawl space, just inside the access window. He scrambled toward his grandfather on all fours, butt in the air, like some misproportioned animal, and peered past him into the stone chamber. "What're you doing?"

Elder held the light to the side, bathing the boy's face with it. "How long you been down here?"

"I was looking for you. Then I heard something and got a little scared." Squatting there, the boy gazed around at the loose rubble, the drill and crowbar, the displaced stones.

"Your daddy going to skin you, find out you been down in this mess."

"It was my dad showed me this hideout, when he was working in here, insulating. He said it could be a place to go, just in case."

"In case what?"

"Case anybody come for us."

"Who would come for you?"

The boy looked away. "Racists. Drug dealers."

The old man couldn't speak for a moment. "Your daddy say that?"

"Maybe Jerome's friends."

"Well." Elder didn't know who Jerome was, some troublemaker in the neighborhood, he thought. "Well," he said again. He felt his certainties unsettled and ajar, a novel, unpleasant feeling. "Case of fire," he said, "house on fire, you come here then?"

"No sir. House on fire, he say get outside, go to the neighbors."

Elder looked at the boy, squatting quietly, looking around. "Why're you here now? Somebody come for you now?"

"No sir. My mom sent me home to bring you over to school. We're going to have some lunch at the carnival. I looked all over the house, and then I come down and saw that screen open." He looked at Elder. "You wearing my dad's clothes?"

The old man studied his grandson's face. It was as if he had never seen it before, though he had known it almost from birth. "I had to borrow some of your daddy's clothes to work back here."

"You done?"

"Yes," he said. "Your daddy have to finish it."

They would be all right. A hiding place beneath the floor was not Elder's idea of a security plan, any more than plastic wrap was his idea of a storm window. But Isaiah was a good father. They would be all right.

"Well," Elder said, "what're we waiting for?"

The boy went ahead of him toward the light of the small window, again moving on hands and feet, protecting his good clothes from the dirt floor. The old man crawled behind him.

SUCH FIRE

I was thinking about Roy, which was not his real name but what he had told me to use when I talked about him. He assumed I would talk about him. "Roy what?"

He had considered for a moment. "Roy Qantas."

"Always the Australian thing."

"Ya gotta problem with that, mate?"

I was at Cannon Lake in western Minnesota, north of Fergus Falls, suffocating from longing and boredom after three days in that cabin. I was thinking about Roy, thinking that he was the one who should have been there, not me. He would have thought to bring along a few bottles of wine, for starters. Maybe a good scotch. More importantly, he was the one who loved playing cards, whereas I have a hard time even remembering the rules. Cards are clumsy in my hands, it's like shuffling pancakes.

I could see Roy dealing, cigar twisting his mouth into a wry half-smile, baseball cap shielding his eyes from the cabin's overdone fluorescent light. More at home than I dancing at the Park or the Gay 90's, he was equally at ease in straight company, and older men charmed him. He could talk sports. He was good at darts. But I was the one my brother-in-law, Walt Duggan, had invited to make the fourth that long weekend at his ancestral cabin, and I had been too shy or too proud or too lazy to ask about a fifth. Something. And now I had ventured out of the cabin into the frigid woods, thinking about Roy, and suffered a vision of youth and desire and mortality.

These men had been going up there every spring for years—Walt, my sister's six foot four, three hundred pound second husband; Richard Miles, an architect, one of Walt's A.A. buddies; and Isaiah Crown, a high school teacher who lived next door to Walt and Rita. A relative newcomer to the group, Isaiah had replaced a heart attack victim a few years before. I myself was replacing a guy who had just died from lung cancer. That was part of the problem, they smoked like a tire dump, and after a few days stuck inside with them, my clothes and skin and hair and sleeping bag reeked of it.

Actually, Isaiah didn't smoke, except for an occasional, sociable cigar, but Walt was as large as two men and smoked like three. I imagined his lungs sometimes as coal burning furnaces, ash-clogged, the cast iron of his huge torso glowing in the darkness. He was a fine, generous man, but it was disconcerting to be closed in with him, even in that big old cabin, two stories sprawled over the crest of Cannon Lake's steep western shore, and after four years it was still weird thinking of him with my sister, though I thought he made her happy.

It was supposed to be a fishing trip, the trout opener, and I had been looking forward to it, pleased that he had invited me. Roy and I occasionally rented a boat and fished for bass or walleye on the St. Croix. I had never fished for trout, though, and had always wanted to learn to fly cast, which seemed a more elegant, romantic kind of fishing, something I could share with Roy afterwards.

But ever since we arrived it had been cold, barely above freezing, the sky leaden from morning to night. When we had pulled away from Walt and Rita's house in St. Paul, it had been a lovely spring morning. Now stray snowflakes drifted aimlessly outside the cabin's wavy-paned windows, floating among the branches of sketchy birches and, I don't know, pines.

They weren't surprised by the dour weather. None of them seemed disappointed. We had bought licenses and beautiful trout stamps in Fergus Falls on the way up, and odds and ends of tackle, but Richard was the only one besides me who brought his fishing gear in from the truck when we pulled up behind the cabin. While Isaiah and I loaded groceries into the old refrigerator and Walt went outside to check the valve on the propane tank, Richard set up a fly-tying jig on the scarred wooden arm of an easy chair and screwed around with feathers and thread, spinners, tiny hooks. Richard was the one who was going to teach me to fly cast. A tall, hunched man with a gaunt face, he was a certified expert and had fished all over the world—northern Canada, Alaska, Scotland, Norway. He had custom-made bamboo fly rods in aluminum cases, the tubes themselves beautifully crafted, lashed together with harness leather straps into a burnished, professional-looking bundle. I arranged my little stash of tackle in a corner, but was too shy to take my estate sale fiberglass fly rod out of its vinyl case.

After sorting out the fly-tying gear, Richard grabbed a few magazines from the stack of *New Yorkers* by the fireplace and settled down at the formica table in the kitchen area of the cabin's log-raftered main floor. Isaiah was already at the table, a book spread open before him. Before turning a page, he would graze his fingers lightly over the print he had just read, as if scanning Braille. Fine-boned, serious-looking in tortoise shell glasses, he seemed to read all the time when we were at the cabin, fat hardcover biographies from the public library, and there was a sort of bubble around him, not just of race, though partly that. I wondered if there was any way to crawl up inside it, get to know him. He concentrated on his book.

All three of them were serious readers, in fact, which surprised me for some reason. Once he had finished poking the cabin into rough order, Walt hauled out a history of Russia and sprawled with it on an ancient mohair sofa, a rusty ashtray resting on his substantial stomach, for the black, fuse-like little cigars he pretty much chain smoked.

I had a mystery and a bunch of case files I had stuck in my suitcase to ease my conscience for taking an unscheduled vacation, from Roy as much as from my work. Stiff from two hours in the cramped back seat of Walt's king cab, however, I didn't feel like reading, so I pulled on my jacket and walked through last year's leaves along the steep path that zigzagged down to the lake, the irregular steps swimming beneath my first pair of bifocals, still dizzyingly new to me. At the bottom of the path there was a narrow, weathered dock and a boathouse covered with green roll roofing. Through a small window I could see a dented aluminum boat resting on rollers, but the doors were locked. When I stepped out onto the dock, it trembled underneath my feet. Flinty water smacked against its pilings with sharp slapping sounds and pushed bits of foam and twigs against the shore. Nature gathered in my blur line as if some perverse magnetism drew it there.

There was another cabin about two hundred feet farther down the shore, newer, more house than cabin, its windows dark. In the other direction, the bay curved into a long, wooded point. Looking back from the end of the dock, I could barely see the roof of Walt's cabin among the trees. Smoke curled from the chimney—somebody had gotten the fireplace going. I shivered in the wind, felt lonely, self-pitying. I clumped back along the swaying dock and climbed up to the cabin, following the heavy smell of wood smoke and the glow from inside that made the afternoon seem darker and colder than ever, the cabin a refuge against the wilderness. And then the comfortable, musty scent of old wood and semi-retired furniture inside, middle-aged men, cigar and cigarette smoke, coffee brewing in a huge, battered percolator.

Walt cooked supper—pork steaks and gravy and biscuits and green beans, honey on the biscuits for dessert. Every meal was like that. Pancakes and fried eggs and plates of bacon for breakfast. Sandwiches of thick-sliced thuringer and cheese on rye bread. A meatloaf crowned with bacon strips. Brownies and cobblers and runny ice cream from the little freezer compartment. Walt did all the cooking, and the rest of us took turns washing the dishes in water hauled up from the pump outside and heated on the stove, dealing however we could with the blankets of grease that swathed every pot and pan and plate. A glass of wine would have helped, but Alcoholics Anonymous seemed to have long been the prevailing religion of Walt's trout opener weekends. Nobody even talked about it.

That first evening, Isaiah wanted to call home, and I rode along with him as he drove Walt's truck the eight miles or so to a crossroads filling station with a pay phone outside. While he was on the phone, I waited in the truck and watched the attendant inside the station watching Isaiah, coming up to the glass doors and staring at Isaiah and looking occasionally in the direction of the truck. Unable to see me clearly in the darkness of the parking lot, he probably assumed I was black, too. I was going to make a joke about the station attendant's nervousness when Isaiah got back to the truck, but he seemed preoccupied. "Everything okay?" I asked.

"Sure," he said, "they're great." He started the truck and swung onto the road. "Sara's expecting, and I wasn't sure I should come up this year, but she said I should." Then he told me what his son had been telling him, a rambling, pointless story that was the main reason he had been on the phone so long.

"You must be a great dad," I said after Isaiah stopped, realizing that he had lost the thread of his kid's story.

"Well," he said. "Yeah, I'm pretty good. You got any kids? You or your partner?"

I looked at him, the line of his jaw under mahogany skin, a handsome, lean face that was difficult to read. I tried to remember what I might have said about Roy on the way up to the cabin.

Isaiah's eyes changed behind the round lenses of his glasses, a look of alarm. "Sorry, is that an offensive question?"

"No," I said, "of course it's not offensive. Neither of us has kids."

"Okay," he said, still uncomfortable. "Because I didn't mean to give offense." He lapsed into silence, and I wanted to reach over and touch his arm.

"It's sweet, actually. Your question."

"Well," he said, and after a while, "Okay, then."

I laughed, and felt as if I had found a friend, though there wasn't very much to say then, and back in the cabin again the dense old air dimmed the sense of connection I had started to feel.

The weather kept its heavy foot on us. Our second night, the propane gas heater conked out, and from then on we had to keep the fireplace going for warmth. We read our books and paged through the old magazines, took naps, ate, drank coffee and soft drinks, threw darts, played dominoes and cards, listened to a ball game on the ancient radio, talked politics. We were all lefty, more or less, and the arguments were ingrown and tepid. I would sometimes notice Walt poking at the coals, trying to stir something up, asking Isaiah about Louis Farrakhan or Jesse Jackson, making remarks about gay marriage for my benefit, but it was as if there wasn't enough oxygen in the cabin, the roaring fireplace drew it off, leaving us—with our unwashed bodies, our unshaven faces, our greasy meals—always a little short of breath, older than we really were.

Playing darts with Isaiah the morning of our second full day of this, I asked him what he taught. History, he said. He told me about the new school he had been transferred to that year, where students stayed with a core group of teachers for several years. "I'll bet you're what we used to call crush bait," I said.

He seemed startled by the idea. "Not me, I'm a hard nose."

"What's that got to do with it?"

"I'm not the kind of teacher pals it up with his students."

"That's not what I meant," I said. "Kids see through that crap." Though I hadn't always. "I mean a smart, good looking, understanding teacher."

He stood there with the three darts resting in the palm of his hand. He was willing to think about it. Finally he shook his head. "Maybe when I was younger."

"What are you, all of thirty-five?"

"Forty-two."

I was three years older. I watched him as he aimed and threw the darts. There was a touch of gray at his temples, but his skin was tight, unlined even in the hollow of his throat. "Let me tell you something," I said, taking my place at the line someone had marked on the scarred wooden floor with electrical tape. "Don't count on old age protecting you for another decade or so." He laughed, flattered, as I wanted him to be, and not as embarrassed as he might have been.

At lunch, Walt kept prodding Richard about getting on with our fly-casting lessons. I thought we could go down to the dock and just cast out into the lake, but Richard said the wind across the open water would push the line right back into our faces. Finally he and I piled some rods and boots and fishing vests into the back of Walt's truck and drove around to some of the sheltered places where we were going to fish if the weather ever lightened a little—mostly bridges where roads crossed the Upper Crow River, the stream we were supposed to be fishing, where you could get down to the water.

This part of western Minnesota is potato country, flat and dull except for the glacial lakes and a few streams choked with brush, and the bridges we stopped at were usually no more than big culverts to carry the gravel roads from one stretch of field to another. The afternoon was still bitterly cold. We scrambled down to the river at one point, leaving the fishing gear in the truck, and Richard explained how he would work along the shore and what kind of fly and what kind of line he would use. After a few minutes we climbed back up to the warm truck and he drove around to a few other nondescript spots, but we didn't get out again. Roman-nosed in profile beneath the long-billed hat he wore indoors and out, he smoked Players and talked about salmon fishing in Scotland and Alaska, and about a job his firm was bidding, and about a house in Minnetonka he was building for himself, and I told him a little about the social service agency I ran in St. Paul, and while we headed back to the cabin we listened to country music on the truck's radio.

Walt was lying down, reading, and Isaiah was reading at the table. A huge log roared in the fireplace, the ghosts of kindling and lesser logs strewn around it, spilling out onto the hearth. Walt looked at Richard and then at me and started to say something, then grunted a little and turned back to his reading.

"What?" I said.

"How'd it go?"

Richard had grabbed a fresh pack of cigarettes and gone out again, headed, I guess, to the outhouse. "Way too cold and windy," I said, rubbing my hands in front of the fire. I looked over, and saw Walt watching me. "What?" I said again. He went back to his reading. An idea occurred to me then. He had been thinking that maybe I would hit it off with Richard, who, now that I thought about it, might have been gay, but who was the kind of man so completely uninvolved romantically that sexual orientation really doesn't matter. This, of course, makes his friends regard him as a challenge, a project. Well, I thought, sorry.

I lay on the plastic-covered bunk bed and wrote a troubled letter to Roy in my head until I dozed off. The previous night I had lain awake for hours listening to Walt's thunderous snoring, and had understood then why Isaiah and Richard had claimed the beds downstairs, in what had looked to me like a storm cellar, musty and dark. Walt was this massive presence across the dark, flickering room, the white knit fabric of his long underwear stretched tight as sails across his thick shoulders and chest and stomach. Even before he started snoring, his vast breathing filled the darkness. I thought about Rita sleeping in the same bed with him.

When we first came into the cabin, Walt had dumped Isaiah's bag on this bunk and directed me downstairs, before Isaiah switched with me. "You mind?" Isaiah had said. "I'm used to that bed downstairs."

"No," I said, "this is great," and watched his smooth, close-cropped head disappear down the stairs. At the time, I thought it might have had to do with the guy who had died, whose bed this must have been. I'm not squeamish about that sort of thing, not any more.

When I woke now, it was almost supper, the smell of hash-browns and onions frying in bacon grease, and coffee, and two more big logs roaring and snapping in the fireplace. For a long time, until Walt called us to the table, I couldn't open my eyes or move myself, there was something thick and sluggish pushing slowly through my veins in place of blood, and even that wasn't circulating, just rolling back and forth, like a muddy tide.

The torpor hung on through supper, clung to me afterward while I scraped at the scum of gravy from the chicken fried steak Walt had cooked in one of the cabin's monstrous cast iron skillets, too wide to fit into the graywater sink or the plastic dishpan full of steamy detergent. When I was finished, Walt took the deck of cards off its designated ledge and we settled into a game of hearts. This time Walt and I were a team, and I was the last to notice that he had been humming "Moon River" while I was struggling to dump the Queen of Spades. And before that probably "Blue Moon." I was so awful, there was an unspoken agreement you could do that, try to cheat if you were my partner

When it was my turn to deal, my grease and dishwater softened fingertips fumbled with the cards, couldn't get them to fan and flutter into a reasonable shuffle.

"No hurry," Walt said. "We got all night."

That was what it felt like. I jammed one half of the deck into the other half a few times and got through the game. By the time we tallied hearts, though, I had to get out. I pulled on my jacket, stepped outside into the still, cold darkness, and shuffled my way up the path toward the outhouse. Halfway there, I decided the hell with it, stepped off the path, and urinated downhill, listening to the thin hiss and patter against invisible dry leaves.

I considered taking Walt's truck and driving over to the filling station and calling Roy. He wouldn't have been home, though. I would just have to leave a message on the machine. I'm alone in the woods with these three men, I would say. Wish you were here. Or, You're not home pining for me, darling boy? Are you having fun already?

He would be, I didn't have to call to know that. I was thinking about Roy when I I heard something moving in the darkness below. The path down to the lake had a handrail along its first run of steps. Silently I felt my way along it as far as I could and peered down to the glassy lake glittering with a thin runner of reflected moonlight. There was a louder noise from below, a brief clatter, voices. I didn't move. Then I could see them down by the dock—teenagers, it sounded like, laughing, messing around on the dock and beside the boathouse. A girl, maybe three or four boys. Their faces glowed briefly in the flare of a match, and the red specks of cigarettes appeared and disappeared.

I watched them, and for a while the weight that had been pressing down on me lifted a little in the clear, cold air. The stink of us, our middle-aged farts and sweat and breath. Receding hair, thickening waists, failing eyes, narrowing possibilities.

The kids were drinking—there was that blur in their laughter, and I thought I could hear the muted clink of aluminum cans in the still night. My lips felt dry. The boys' voices were self-consciously deep, still unfamiliar to them, and the girl had a careless teasing manner, as if one of the boys were her brother. I heard somebody softly rattle the door knob of the boathouse, and I waited for the sound of breaking glass. Instead, a figure suddenly appeared on the shallow sloping roof, vaguely outlined against the glittering water, dancing clumsily, urging the others to join him. The girl called something mocking up at him, and a can clattered down the roof, and after a few moments he leaped into the darkness. I heard the explosion of his breath as he hit the ground, and sharp, barking laughter. A match flared. Somebody pushed close to it, lighting a cigarette, and then another, and somebody cursed and dropped the match, and the others laughed.

They moved off, finally, and after a while the breathless cold sank unbearably through my jacket and I had to go in. Walt was playing solitaire, and the others were reading, Richard with his stockinged feet propped on the hearth, Isaiah across the table from Walt's shifting ranks of cards. Walt looked up at me. "Thought you might have gotten lost. I was about to send the boys out looking for you."

"The wind's pretty much died down," I said. "It might be nice enough tomorrow we could go fishing."

Walt studied his cards, turned one over. "If the wind's stopped, it's going to get cold as hell."

It did, too. I had to pull my sleeping bag hood tight over my face that night, and in the morning nobody got up until it had been fully light for an hour or two. Frost crystals glittered on the log walls. We fed the fireplace as if it were a ravenous beast. After lunch I finished my mystery, shuffled through the case files I had brought along, wrote another letter to Roy, a real one this time, then put on my jacket. "Anybody want to go for a walk?" I asked. "Isaiah, how about a little fresh air?" For a second I thought he was interested, but then he looked out over the skeletal birches and the bleak expanse of water and shook his head.

"You don't have a real coat, do you?" Walt asked. "Take mine, you're going to freeze your ass. Take my hat and gloves."

"It's not so bad," I said, but put on his big leather gloves and tucked his stocking cap into a pocket. I stepped outside, then went back in and pulled Walt's enormous sheepskin coat on over my jacket.

The woods were dense with brush around there, and the fields were plowed up, spiky with old corn stubble, uninviting even if I could have seen what was under my own feet through the bifocals. Ponderous in the stiff sheepskin, I hiked out to the highway and walked along the dusty shoulder for a while with Walt's cap drawn down over my ears, but after a few trucks blasted past, I got tired of the sick, doomed feeling of redneck metal bearing down on me, and I turned back. It was Sunday. I wondered if there was a chance that I would run into the teenagers from the night before, and how I would look to them in the huge clothes—massive myself, or shrunken and old inside of them. I stuffed Walt's purple and gold Vikings cap back into a coat pocket and felt the suddenly rising wind grab at my hair, yanking it the wrong way back.

At the beginning of the lane turning off to Walt's place, the air already was draped with wood smoke. When I reached the cabin, I looked in a window and saw Walt napping mountainously under an opened sleeping bag and Richard and Isaiah throwing darts at the puffy, water-stained board. For a while I watched them from outside, tasting the creepy mix of jealousy and protectiveness and loneliness. I was thinking about Roy, who was good at darts, who knew how to make the most of whatever time he had, certain of his faithlessness, missing him.

To the east, the lake stretched out grayly beyond the scrim of trees, whitecaps kicking up, trees on the far shore already starting to sink into afternoon shadow. I watched Richard lining up a dart, aiming it as if his life depended on it, adjusting, aiming some more with little feinting motions while Isaiah waited, leaning against the cabin's golden varnished wall.

I eased past the door and clambered down toward the lake. There was a path along the shore leading from the neighboring cabin's dock around the back of the boathouse, which is where the teenagers the night before must have walked. I found myself hunching over, studying the ground for some sign that they had been there, the impression of that boy's body when he struck the ground, or beer cans, or condoms, or underpants. When I noticed a cigarette butt's whiteness against the brown drift of last year's leaves, I lifted it carefully with my thick-gloved thumb and forefinger and dropped it into a coat pocket.

Otherwise, there was no sign they had been there, and I was turning back toward the cabin when I noticed a thin trickle of smoke swirling above the leaf mould, so delicate it could have been a whiff of pollen or mist from the faint warmth of decay, or only the smear of my bifocals' reading lenses. I scraped at the leaves with my shoe and then bent over and separated them carefully with hands made awkward and invulnerable by Walt's oversized gloves. The edge of a leaf glowed suddenly and broke up as the wind caught it. I dropped to my knees and sheltered it with my body while the redness pulsed slowly, as if breathing. I stayed hunched over there, scarcely breathing myself, until a pale flame licked up shyly, and I let my breath out.

It was how you feel when you discover a baby bird or rabbit cowering inches from your lawn mower, the idiotic, futile tenderness that leads you to make a little nest for it of grass clippings, to nudge it toward some shrubbery, superstitiously careful not to touch it, not to taint it with your human smell. You mention it, maybe, in bed that night, wonder about its parents, and wish it well, knowing that some prowling cat will get it, hoping that nothing will be left that you will have to bury.

The tiny fire. I brushed a little nest around it, inside a ring of earth, then took off Walt's gloves and fed the fire a fragment of dry leaf, a spray of orange pine needles, a shred of curling birch bark. The smoke was fragrant and soft, delicate, utterly different from the resinous pall of wood smoke billowing out of the cabin's chimney. Almost invisible in the thin glance of sunlight, the flame trembled with the flutter of a minute heartbeat.

But you don't spend all day with those doomed orphans. After a while I scraped the fire into a fist-sized mound and watched it burn itself out. When it was dead, I scuffed the ashes into the ground with the toe of my shoe and for good measure laid an ungloved palm over the ashy spot, feeling its warmth already fleeing into the cold ground.

Only after I straightened finally did I notice another wisp of smoke threading out of the leaves a few feet away. I stomped on it, but the leaves lay more thickly here and the fire that must have been smoldering since the night before burst up with the impact of my shoes, scattering sparks. I pulled the gloves back on and dropped to my knees and raked the smoking leaves inward, clawing down to the frozen soil, struggling to scrape the fire together with both hands like a miser gathering in spilled gold.

There was too much of it, it had spread outside the reach of my arms, and I wasn't able to scratch much of the frozen earth over the fire that had been waiting all night and day for me. I stamped around a few more times, then ran up the path and stairs to the cabin and burst in and shouted for them to help me, there was a fire down by the lake. Richard ran outside, and Isaiah dashed downstairs to get his coat. Walt sat up in bed and stared at me.

"There's a fire down by the boathouse, it's spreading in the leaves," I said. "You got a shovel? Buckets?"

Richard rushed back in. "Shit, Walt" he shouted, "you've got to see this." Then he was gone again. I grabbed the old ash bucket and shovel from in front of the fireplace, sending the warped, rusty screen crashing to the floor. Walt grunted and swung his legs over the side of the bed and fumbled for his boots. Isaiah hauled out the biggest pots and pans he could find in the kitchen, and we poured out of the cabin and headed down toward the lake.

What had been a patchy mist of smoke rising from the leaves was now a loose cloud floating in the branches of the surrounding woods. We found Richard scraping at the leaf mould with his bare hands. I gave him the little fireplace shovel and he hacked at the ground with it, tossing dirt into the smoke. Still in his undershirt, suspenders flapping, Walt attacked the fire with a dusty rag rug he had dragged down from the entry of the cabin. Isaiah and I scooped up lake water with the ash bucket and kitchen pots and ran up and flung it into the heart of the rolling smoke.

"We've got to contain it," Walt shouted. "Push it down toward the lake." Coughing, swearing, we started to work together, kicking and scraping a fire line to protect the brushy woods and the boat-house. The flames were creeping under the mat of bent grass and dead leaves, so it was hard to judge the perimeter, and we kept cut-ting in too close, only to find smoke rising behind us.

Finally we had it surrounded, though, and gradually worked the fire toward the rocky shore. We called out to each other when we noticed smoke starting to work its way between us, or flaring up where we thought we had smothered it. Sweating, half-blinded by smoke and tears, I flung off the heavy sheepskin coat and felt the welcome push of cold wind against my arms and chest. I couldn't re-member discarding the gloves and hat—they must have been around somewhere. My hands ached and burned from clawing at the weedy, rocky ground. We passed each other coming and going from the dock where we scooped up pans of water. We splashed water over the smoldering edge of the burned area and scraped the soil into a broader and broader swath.

"Starting to look like a brother," Isaiah observed to me once as we passed each other, and when I stopped and turned, confused, he brushed a hand across my cheek.

"Burn, baby, burn!" I said, but he was already heading back to the lake for more water and might not have heard me, or maybe I hadn't said it out loud. We were so tired and pleased with ourselves by then, it didn't matter. The only thing that mattered was getting the job done, that we had saved the woods, the boathouse, the neighbor's deserted and vulnerable house.

Richard, Walt, and I followed Isaiah down toward the lake. As we walked, Walt lit a narrow cigar and handed it to Richard and lit another for himself. He looked at me. I shrugged, and he took the cigar from between his lips and offered it to me. "Come on, hair of the dog." He took a drag and looped one of his huge arms across my shoulders. "You know, Tom," he said, "I think you were starting to get bored up here. I think this was just what you needed."

"Ya gotta problem with that, mate?"

Isaiah was kneeling on the dock, leaning over the edge and scooping another pot full of water to add to the two already beside him. Walt and Richard continued toward the lake, but I stopped and took off my filthy glasses, breathed on the lenses, and tried to clean them with the tail of my shirt. It was starting to get dark. I turned and held the smeared lenses up against the last light of the day. Over the crest of the steep bank, through the screen of scraggly pine and bare birch trees, the sky glowed. Smoke billowed up from Walt's cabin.

I dropped the hand holding the bifocals to my side and stared toward the west with naked eyes. Just out of sight, fire rolled and swelled, gorging itself on old wood floors and varnished timber walls, on musty cotton mattresses, on case files and castoff furniture and handmade bamboo rods, a coffee can of congealed bacon grease, playing cards, an unmailed letter, darts and dart board and sleeping bags. Such fire, I imagined myself telling Roy, I had never seen such fire.

A SMALL, DARK, ROARING MOON

HE SAW THIS once on *Nova*—Egyptian laborers levering an obelisk up while an Englishman tossed pebbles underneath it. They shifted the fulcrum and levered again. More pebbles, more levering, gradually raising one end of the impossibly heavy pillar above the desert floor until finally it could be pulled fully upright with ropes. Isaiah has no laborers, but he has a long iron pry bar, and buckets of rock sifted from the flower bed he has been digging, and a 10 by 12 by 30 inch artifact he discovered at the bottom of his excavation. He thinks it is dressed limestone left over from the pre-Civil War house next door.

Across the street, Somali kids are playing basketball in front of the Withers' garage, lots of cursing, which means Howard isn't home. "*Hell* no!" a boy shouts when somebody shoots, a charm against scoring. Soon others take it up, "*Hell* no!" punctuating the slapping of the ball on pavement and the crash against rickety backboard and the roar and shudder of a helicopter flying somewhere close by.

Where Isaiah is working, between his driveway and the chain link fence surrounding the old stone house, the ground is so full of junk, he has decided to dig everything out, separate the rubble—clinkers, bottles, rocks, chunks of brick, sawed bones—then return the good soil amended with compost. He was about to leave off digging and start backfilling when his shovel struck what turned out to be this block, not much larger than carry-on luggage, but incredibly heavy.

He levers with the pry bar, shoves flat stones under the block. When he straightens to set a new fulcrum, two little Hmong girls are leaning on the fence beneath his dwarf cherry tree. "Mister," one of them says, "are we supposed to eat these fruit?"

He thinks about the question. "They're sour."

"We don't mind," the other one declares.

The girls stand on tiptoe, select a handful each from the low-bend-ing branches, glancing over their shoulders to see how closely he's watching them. A boy chases the basketball across the street, looks over at Isaiah, then grabs some cherries from a branch that is out of reach for the Hmong girls. "Man," he says, "these are *good*," but he doesn't take any more.

The roar of the helicopter has not gone away. Isaiah climbs out and walks into the street, and the basketball players point until he catches sight of it through a gap between tree branches, higher than he expected, and maybe a dozen blocks to the north and west. He waits to see which direction it goes, but though the throbbing seems to advance and recede, the helicopter hangs motionless in the evening sky, as steady as a moon. A small, dark, roaring moon. The Hmong girls run away, leaving a trail of cherries rolling on the sidewalk.

Isaiah would get out his bicycle and ride over to see what's going on that holds the helicopter transfixed, but he has the great block almost to the lip of his hole, pry bar and perilous stack of rubble jammed underneath. On *Nova*, white men are always demonstrating how ancient Egyptians or Maya or Easter Islanders did some difficult thing. Sometimes the theory is ridiculous, like the guy claiming the Inca cut massive stones using the sun's heat concentrated by parabolic golden mirrors, who couldn't even get straw to smolder that way.

The lever and pebble method works fine, however, and as darkness falls Isaiah wrestles the block onto his driveway. He is dead tired, but pleased he managed the feat without crushing any of his extremities or rupturing a disk or having the pry bar spring back and break his jaw.

The helicopter is gone. His friend Lynette tells him about it the next day. A woman had been discovered in a car's trunk, that was why the helicopter was there. Neighbors had noticed the smell, called the police. "I couldn't believe it," Lynette says, "people hanging out of windows, climbing out on their porch roofs, everybody trying to get a look." She shakes her head. "I wouldn't want to look at no dead body in a trunk, poor thing."

"I thought of going over to see what was happening," Isaiah says.

She looks at him. "You did no such thing."

"I thought about it."

"A dead body?"

"I didn't know what it was."

"What it was was a dead body in some murdering fool's trunk."

In the light of day, Isaiah discovers after hosing it off that the block he salvaged with such effort is not stone at all, but concrete. He uses the pry bar to tumble it back into the hole, now dotted with cherries, and buries it again, a pointless secret at the bottom of his new flowerbed's rich, deep soil.

ABOUT THE AUTHOR

Lon Otto has published two previous collections of stories—*A Nest of Hooks* (U. of Iowa Press), winner of the Iowa School of Letters Award for Short Fiction, and *Cover Me* (Coffee House Press)—and the craft chapbook *Grit* (Writers Workshop Press). His writing is in many anthologies, including *The Pushcart Prize* (Pushcart Press), *American Fiction* (New Rivers Press), *Flash Fiction* and *Flash Fiction Forward* (W.W. Norton), *Blink* and *Blink Again* (Spout Press), *Townships* (U. of Iowa Press), *The Runner's Literary Companion* (Breakaway Books), and *Not Normal, Illinois* (Indiana U. Press), as well as the craft text *Best Words, Best Order* (St. Martin's Press). He regularly teaches in the University of Iowa Summer Writing Festival and is professor emeritus at the University of St. Thomas in St. Paul, Minnesota.

Made in the USA
Monee, IL
24 November 2020